Thick, Thin, What The Dragon Let In

Stories, Rhymes, and Reveries

by Doworth Howard

FIERCE PLUM
Williamsburg

ISBN 978-1-956869-00-2 (Paperback Edition)

ISBN 978-1-956869-01-9 (E-Book Edition)

Names: Howard, Doworth, author.

Title: Thick, thin, what the dragon let in : stories, rhymes, and reveries / Doworth Howard.
Description: Williamsburg, VA : Fierce Plum, 2025.

Identifiers: LCCN 2024921895 (print) | ISBN 978-1-956869-00-2 (paperback) | ISBN 978-1-956869-01-9 (ebook) | Also available in ebook and audiobook formats.

Subjects: LCSH: Humorous stories. | Short stories. | Crime stories. | Surrealism. | Poetry. | Song texts. | BISAC: POETRY / Subjects & Themes / General. | POETRY / American / General. | FICTION /

Short Stories (single author)

Classification: LCC PS3558.O93 T53 2025 (print) | LCC PS3558.O93 (ebook) | DDC 813/.6--dc23.

Library of Congress Control Number: 2024921895

This book is entirely a work of fiction. The names, characters and incidents portrayed in it are the work of the author's imagination. Any resemblance to actual persons, living or dead, events or localities is entirely coincidental and not intended by the author.

Printed and bound in the USA
First Printing February 2025
Published by Fierce Plum
Williamsburg
Visit www.fierceplum.com

To Jake

Good luck reading the writing.
Embrace the experimental space.
Or move along jivey polecat.
Stupider by the minute.
But, moderation is for judges.

—Rod Florens

PREFACE

Innovative writing. Is there anything new to do? Surely, it's been written every which way. Diagonally, upside down, right, left, unhinged. Are you looking for a gimmick? An exceptional something that promotes or sells words in a new way? There's serious competition for attention. What sets it apart? Interactivity? Visuals? Social media? Backlash? Disruption? Something old-fashioned, forgotten?

A corpse of literature. Tome of death. Something bound. A replacement of paper that is physical yet resource light. Is it electric? A tablet? Blah!

No, it's the medium that needs something different. They styled the words. The fonts. No, deeper. More meaning, and shock and awe. That's old.

Dig deep for something genuinely exciting about words. Projections of words. On a screen? Big or small? Silver?

The one word at a time lasted a second. Bold, underline. No, it's in the plot or the parting of the words. Spaces? Avant Garde? No, less vomit-inducing. Even or odd questions like? It could be three. Pause and move for a bit. Something to do with some thing?

No, in that it's an idea that takes shape only when certain words and phrases appear. A maze of words? Sentences within sentences? No, not anagrams either, not that or them.

A new way to read words. But it is the substance. Yes, not the style. Then is it a new plot device? How a character is created? A new kind of universe and world? A new folk legend for modernity, but that's old. Replacements for vampires and werewolves. A new fantasy to capture two imaginations. Can't be forced. It must be relatable. Stir ourselves.

Connected to the truth. No doubt.

So, if it is in the substance, what's the new genre? A whole new empire. But what? Maybe its derived from a sickness or a virus or the Internet. An old-world entity reborn to a new odd time?

It's got to be cool. Capture the imagination, sure. There must be rules. *Jabberwocky.* Look that up. Not *Highlander.* Not return of some spirit or *Evil Dead.* Not that that's not good enough, but no *Bubba Ho-Tep* either. Seriously serious stuff on a higher plain or plane. But no bullshit! It's a mostly meek human experience never quite captured before. Quite right?

ACKNOWLEDGEMENTS

Special thanks to Brad, Samir and Mindy, Kyle and Kristen, Antoine and Masha, Mike and Laura, Jon, the Rejected Writers Group (you know who you are), Rod and Wynne, anonymous, mobsters on the sidelines validating street credit, and especially all in the fam and the band, plus me olde studio mates.

A CUP OF COFFEE

"You don't want any cream or sugar?" Clancy asked Chuck after being served coffee by a waitress at Nick's Diner off the Ditmars stop in Astoria, Queens.

"I like my coffee like I like my women," Chuck said.

"How's that?"

"Hot and black."

Clancy chuckled. "I guess I like my ladies sweet and creamy then. But seriously what the hell can we do?"

"I know," Chuck said shaking his head before blowing on his coffee. "We have to come up with fifty large by Saturday night and all because of that douche Milos fucking us over."

"That doesn't matter now," Clancy said. "We'll deal with Milos if we get out this hole. Getting 50k to the Denali Brothers keeps us alive and that's all we need to think about doing. I don't know how we're going to do it."

"What can we do to get that kind of money? Who, what, where can we score fifty grand from like now?" Chuck asked before taking his first sip.

"I got nothing," Clancy said.

"My cousin Jermaine has a security job at the Museum of Modern Art. Maybe he would let us in and we take a piece of fine art and sell it."

"What do we know about art? And besides art is the stuff you have to let cool, lay low. That would be a big heist in the news at a place like MOMA. And we'd have to find a buyer."

"I got my boy, Trevor, who is hustling over in the Diamond District, maybe he knows how some jewels could go missing."

"Everyone knows everyone over there, and we'd have to go up to Canada, somewhere far, to sell whatever we get, so no one in the city knows and there's no time."

Both took sips from their mugs contemplating.

"What about a bank?" Chuck said.

"Nah, I've robbed banks before," Clancy said. "If you want to do a quick and easy, in and out robbery with one teller, you get like what? A few grand at most. That's too many banks to rob. If we go for the big score, with heavy guns and everything for the kind of cash we need, then we'd have to worry about cops giving a damn and being all over our asses fast. Plus, there's the risk of the whole dye pack shit and I don't want to have to kill anyone over this bullshit, except Milos maybe."

"All right," Chuck said leaning forward cupping his cup. "I know this guy Carlos who is in deep with this Mexican crew that slings meth and coke. I bet we could give him some cabbage to get his fix and he'd show us a safe house and look the other way. Those safe houses always got mad money. We scope it out and hit it up fast."

Contemplating, Clancy took a big gulp of his coffee and then said, "Do you want to get in trouble with another crew that we know nothing about or who they are in order to pay the Denalis? We don't know what they are in to or who they're connected to. Those bastard Denalis have their fingers in everything. For all we know, we'd be robbing one of their outfits to pay them back, and we'd be even more fucked than we are now, which is already fucked."

"There's a big party at Cipriani's with a lot of singers and celebrities for some fundraiser for kids with cancer. They must have some cash and jewelry to take."

"Too big and high profile. Hard to control the crowds and not get noticed. Plus, it's kids with cancer."

"Fine Mr. Morality," Chuck said and drank deep.

"We must be overlooking something," Clancy said.

"What about that strip club where Linda works? She could let us in at the end of her shift and we get the manager to take us to the safe. He's a dummy anyway, right? There's got to be some serious loot moving in and out of that club."

"Absolutely not," Clancy said. "I don't want Linda involved. I owe her two-months child support and she won't be in to robbing no boss. Plus, they got some heavy bouncers on Friday nights I wouldn't mess with. They are some mean sons of bitches. Once I saw them break a guy's nose for rubbing up against some stripper's titties too long."

"I got a guy I've known since high school who's out at the Aqueduct, Cowboy Steve. He usually has a good line on the horses. We could talk to him. Get into the horses good, you know, and see what we can win on. Maybe hit a few trifectas. Plus, they got that casino out there."

"My luck is decent, but it ain't that good. Christ with the odds of any bets working, we'd be better off buying a bunch of lottery tickets."

"Damn son, what's with the negativity?" Chuck said pushing his cup aside. "I mean, Clancy, here I am coming up with all of these ideas to get us out of this shit, which ain't easy. And all you've got is negativity with everything. Stop it man. We need some positive waves up in here or we're dead. Don't be so negative and say no to everything. Besides what the hell kind of ideas do you have that are so great to be shooting down every damn one I got?"

"You know I know you're right man, but I don't know," Clancy said looking at his empty cup, shaking his head.

"We best get thinking," Chuck said finishing his cup.

"I need another coffee," Clancy said and nodded to the waitress for a refill.

"Me too."

"Black, right?" the waitress said to Chuck.

"You know it."

Rando if you don't know (I)

SUSPICIOUS

Suspicious, vicious fishes make delicious, nutritious dishes.

AND YOU

Something evil and nimble comes
Something evil and nimble comes, again
Go get your friend
Whipping wind
Then tapping tin
Clattering around the bend
From way up there on the other side
Wait too late for your pride
And you
Feathers left of birds and shells of turtles
Mists don't resist nor tempt the wicked too
And you
All that's left is your loose screw
And maybe that suede shoe
And you.

THE HUN AND THE VANDALS

"Stop kicking that sculpture. It's a piece of art that someone obviously spent a lot of time on and what did it ever do to you?" Serge said.

"Fuck man, c'mon let's break some more shit!" Mickey said. "I'm feeling it."

Serge wondered how he got dragged into the whole affair as his friend recklessly pulverized a bronze-colored porcelain statue of a wild stallion. They stood in the foyer of some strange guy's house. A guy Serge never knew or cared anything about. Yet for some reason Mickey convinced Serge that this was the home of the guy who picked on Mickey in high school. Some big jock douche named Ted.

Apparently, Mickey saw Ted the other day and followed him back to this house. A sense of rage overtook Mickey as he recounted the taunts and abuses he'd received from Ted during his miserable dork days of high school.

"That jizz whiz gave me a wedgie calling me Crapster every damn day for two years."

Sitting at a cheap happy hour bar earlier in the evening, Mickey persuaded a rather buzzed Serge to assist in exacting revenge.

A more sober Serge now assessed the situation. Broken objects of various shapes and forms dotted the white shag carpet in the living room. Serge looked down and noticed they had tracked mud across the carpet. Their previous paces and close stutter steps made to pummel or shatter a tough object, such as the glass coffee table and the vases on the brick mantel above the faux fireplace, remained.

Serge felt he had contributed little to the havoc wrought all over the house, but he'd still be indicted just the same. What were they thinking? They were professionals in their mid-thirties not stupid punk kids out for jollies and destruction.

Serge began to regret being there. He speculated if he had stayed with Brenda, instead of dumping her over some bullshit commitment issue then perhaps he would be married and home with his wife, dinner waiting, and queue the happy Golden Retriever named Sparky and the cutesy three-year-old toddler named Todd running to greet him.

No, instead he lingered in the middle of anything but domestic bliss.

"Mickey, we should leave, we've done enough," Serge demanded. "Let's go!"

"Don't be such a pussy," Mickey replied. "You barely broke anything besides the lock. Plus, there's a mirror above the bed upstairs. I want to bust that up before we go. And did you see that aquarium? I should dump the fish out on the floor with the water. Ted can watch them gasp for air when he's all freaked out by his wrecked house. God, I haven't felt so alive in years. Do you feel that adrenaline man?"

"Can't say I do anymore. Don't be a sicko Mickey. Leave the fish alone. Look, I want to go. The longer we're here the better chance we have of getting caught. I can't believe you convinced me to come here."

"Not my fault if you're too weak-minded bro," Mickey said before pulling down a bookshelf. "Screw reading. Am I right?"

"Says the web editor."

Frustrated and feeling like an idiot, Serge wanted to tell Mickey he was leaving when he heard keys opening the front door.

Crap, Serge thought and alerted Mickey to be silent crouching and motioning towards the door. Mickey gulped and with careful pantomiming motions suggested that they sneak upstairs.

"WHAT THE FUCK!" Ted screamed entering his house. A big sports fan, Ted was already irritated at having seen his football team lose by six touchdowns earlier and now this. Ted stomped around with his hulking body. His skin tone turned bright red offsetting his spiky blonde hair and crystal blue eyes. His breathing accelerated to an animalistic pace of rage. Ted stalked the lower level of his home kicking the various destroyed items in his way.

Serge and Mickey managed to make their way upstairs without Ted hearing.

In a bedroom, they found a window near a tree. Mickey softly suggested they open the window and jump to the tree then work their way down to freedom. Carefully, Mickey unlocked the window and slid it open.

A detachable reinforced storm screen impeded their progress. Mickey reached at the different corners to remove it but unfastened the last part the wrong way and lost hold of the heavy screen and it crashed to the ground. Mickey and Serge paused thinking Ted didn't hear the sound giving each other a sigh.

But then suddenly Ted charged up the stairs yelling various obscenities, threatening death.

"Go, go, jump," Mickey yelled to Serge. "He's coming, go, Jesus!"

Serge's heart pulsed as he put half of his body out the window. He tried to reach the tree, but it was too far. He fell hard. His knee hurt severely from taking the fall's impact. He lay on his back grasping his knee. He saw Mickey above climbing out the window looking to jump. Serge expected to be crushed. But in a quick jerking motion Mickey stopped before he started.

"Come here, motherfucker!" Ted yelled grabbing Mickey's hoody top as he jumped out the window. Ted held Mickey in midair with his pulsing beefy forearms trying to pull Mickey back up into the house. Mickey screamed. Serge continued to writhe in pain and watch. Ted pulled Mickey up slightly and began choking him. Mickey's spindly legs flailed.

Seeing Mickey grow weaker with slowing legs and flatlining features, Serge knew he had to save him. He hobbled fast as possible to the front of the house, opened the door, and made his way upstairs.

In the bedroom, he saw Ted leaning out the window still choking Mickey.

Serge had no other recourse than to go for the legs. With superhero-like might, Serge grabbed Ted's ankles. Ted kicked and flailed, but in vain. In a quick motion, Serge forced Ted out the window.

Serge couldn't see what happened, but somehow all the momentum must have caused Mickey and Ted to flip in the air because, when Serge looked out, Mickey lay atop Ted, as though Mickey had pinned Ted like a wrestler.

Serge rushed downstairs and outside. In pain, Mickey screamed. Ted appeared unconscious. Serge checked that Ted kept a pulse and steady breath.

The impact may have been hard on Ted, but he looked like a surviving ox, Serge decided. Serge picked up Mickey and struggled to carry him back to the car.

Serge plopped Mickey in the passenger side, revved up the car and sped off.

As they drove away Mickey began to recover.

"Wow what a rush, that was crazy. That big motherfucker nearly made me shit my pants," Mickey exclaimed.

"Think you got your revenge?"

"No, I realized that wasn't Ted."

Rando if you don't know (1.5)

THE DUCK AND THE CAT

Holding a mallard. Taking water from a white cat on snowy riverbanks, as part of some team survival, scavenger get to the next level game. Not many supplies. Find them along the way. Like a pair of white sneakers with bright blue stripes, slightly hidden in sandy banks. Put them on. Hope they fit. Run and follow the duck and cat: getting ready for something . . .

TREASURE ROBBER

A fractured skull emerged through the shifting dirt as Gerald deftly managed the shovel. He needed to ensure he missed nothing. Careful and steady, but fast. Daylight threatened. The security guards, despite their general stupor, would be more observant with the light. He should have left already. He'd been up all night searching for the plot on this ancient land. The local who'd sold him the map was correct. The bodies were here. Too sacred for the local man to destroy, Gerald paid no concern with the promise of gold and exotic stones. Heavy items created by forgotten artisans, all belonging in a museum, but ideally sold and fenced to someone else to do with what they liked, perhaps a private collection or a smelter. Gerald didn't care. Bottom line was the promise of money and a new life.

HIT ME

On a coast in a land by the beach the waves crash with a mighty roar. A man in a tuxedo sits on the coarse sand alone looking towards the ocean taking a pull from an overpriced bottle of bubbly. Occasionally, he takes a puff from a big fat cigar gnawed and wet at the tip. His thoughts run deep wondering why. Toiling repeatedly the previous night's events. He cannot find an answer to his actions. How could he have killed that giraffe?

The night before in the casino, the man sat at the blackjack table down $1500 thanks to a bad streak of poorly planned double downs, busted cards, and overly cautious stays on fifteen. Sipping on a free scotch and soda, he chewed heartily on a chunk of ice, pondering his decision. He had an eight showing and ten underneath, but his confidence waned and he expected the dealer had a better hand.

Hit or stay, hit or stay, he thought. The other players grew agitated by his indecision and stared at him in disgust. The man remained tranquil, hit or stay. The dealer coughed in an attempt to prod the man into action. The man looked up swallowing the melted remnants of the ice cube.

"Hit me."

The dealer slapped the card on the table. Seven. Damn. There went another $250.

The man left the table in an unpleasant mood heading towards the bar. He ordered another Scotch and soda and turned around to look at the people milling about the bustling casino. He quickly knocked back his drink and another and another.

Noticing the man's expensive watch and tailored tux, a call girl approached. They chatted, aware of each other's deeper motivations. Hers was money and his was the need to get lucky on a losing night even if he had to pay for it.

After a required amount of dialogue, it was agreed that the girl should go back to the man's suite.

Inside, the man popped open a bottle of chilled champagne offering the call girl a flute to warm the spirit. Soon the girl was naked on the bed ready to go.

They completed their business transaction, and the girl asked the man if she could shower. While the girl bathed, the man went out onto his balcony that over-looked the enclosed safari park within the casino. Several dismal exotic creatures lay caged, like elephants, lions, and flamingos. The man recalled that the casino built the safari park a few years back in hopes of attracting more of a family crowd. But how many decent parents think of taking their children to a casino to look at malnourished creatures from foreign lands?

The man lit a cigar and watched the slow pounding walk of an elephant. A sign said don't feed the animals.

Later the call girl came out refreshed and ready to go back to work. There was the matter of the bill. The man reached for his wallet and pulled out $200.

That wasn't the agreed upon price, the girl said.

Words grew to shouts and as the girl grabbed at the man's wallet a struggle ensued. The girl began to slap and punch. Unaware of his strength, the man shoved her away. She ran back towards him and this time he shoved harder.

The force of the push knocked the girl backwards then over the low railing.

Stunned briefly, the man ran over to the railing hearing loud screams of horror coming from the flying girl. The man watched as she fell inside the safari park. Then a loud bestial noise rang out. The sound of a huge thud emanated throughout the park stirring the other creatures to call out in their various shrieks of excitement.

The man stared at the ground and heard the call girl cry. She was alive, but in pain. However, the giraffe that broke her fall lay below, dead from a broken neck.

Attendants raced out to see what happened with a crowd of gawkers quickly gathering.

Realizing what he had done, the man grabbed the bottle of champagne and left the casino quickly by catching a taxi. The man remained uncertain as to where to go and finally told the cabbie to drop him off at the beach.

The man spent the rest of the night listening to the waves and pondering his misfortune. As the sun began to rise, he stubbed out his cigar and took one last pull from the bottle. The man got up and tossed the champagne bottle high up in the air towards the ocean.

A sudden bang came from behind before the bottle shattered. Bewildered, the man turned around to see two policemen with pistols trained on his body.

BLACK

Fifty-seven minutes to dawn, a man wearing all black emerged from a darkened street in Hell's Kitchen.

He wore a balaclava that masked his face and opaque aviator sunglasses to hide any expression. Atop his head a skullcap and a heavy hood covered his head, creating deep shadows. A long trench coat, black jeans, gloves, and combat boots completed his dark ensemble.

With a black backpack strapped tight to his back, he rolled behind him a small piece of carry-on luggage, oddly pink, handcuffed to his left wrist.

He walked quickly wondering if he'd gotten away with his misdeeds. Oh, the deep pleasure he took. He felt a lovely sense of exhilaration. His heart raced. Several times he paused to look back ensuring no one followed. Soon he came upon Times Square. The brightness from the numerous lights overhead and the bustling people looking to start their day or end their night made him nervous. Yet, he felt empowered as never before. He could do what he wanted if need be.

Even for New York, he might look conspicuous, but no one paid him any attention, including the cop he nearly bumped into on his way down into the subway.

Struggling with the carry-on down the steps, he grew agitated, but needed it until he could safely toss it. He reached in his jacket pocket for his MetroCard and swiped through the turnstile. He waited patiently for the R train counting the seconds with the rhythmic timing he'd practiced so many times.

The R arrived one thousand three hundred thirty seconds later. He chose an empty front car and took a seat by the door. As the R pulled out the station, he relaxed ever so slightly believing he'd gotten away. He smiled a twisted grin, but there was no one to wonder what the strange man might be musing.

Rando if you don't know (II)

THE LAW

The law is only respected if you believe in it, and usually the law requires fear. If you can get beyond that fear, then you are free to do what you want, at least as the law will allow . . .

ESCAPING PARADISE

After a year of non-stop work and near the end of the big project, Jack Stengel finally took a vacation from his hectic schedule in New York. His secretary, Connie, had suggested Manuel Antonio Beach in Costa Rica. Sure, it was nice and beautiful, but this was Connie's paradise, not Jack's. The calm put him on edge. He simply couldn't get comfortable. The touts kept passing him on the lounge chair asking if he wanted surfing lessons or massages or coconut water or too many other things to count.

It's not as if a more private beach would do him any better. He wasn't a beach person. Nor a mountain person. The jungle behind him with all the squawking sounds of exotic birds, bugs, and monkeys brought him no joy.

Leave your worries behind, Connie had said. He missed his worries. He worried instead about having nothing to worry about temporarily and then a flood of catching up on two weeks of work when he returned. Would the Parsons deal be done? What if the goons screwed everything up while he was away?

No, they'd been trained by him. Surely, they knew what they were doing? No, they probably didn't. Should he call? It might put his mind at rest. Or would it? He didn't want to have a drink. He hadn't for years because it kept his edge, but it could be dangerous too.

Why was that black man looking? The sun beat down. Maybe it was time for more lotion or to flip. The flipping would be easier. Don't you need to burn a bit to get a good base? He should have gone to the tanning salon. Do people do that anymore? Cancer, well everyone would get it.

That's what caused the first attempt at the deal with Parsons to fall through three years ago. The original Mr. Parsons got diagnosed with bone cancer and died within a few weeks. A real shame, he was a titan of industry, and it was too fragile a time to confront the Widow Parsons, although that is exactly what Jack did. Or he'd employed his wife at the time to do that. But everything went incredibly wrong and fell through.

At least with the divorce he deflected the blame to the ex-wife. Parsons' son saw the time for change coming and needed the money. Fentanyl wasn't cheap, lest one was inclined to fall from society. It would be a good deal for all, maybe not the Widow Parsons, but everyone else, especially Jack. But then why had he left before they sealed the deal?

He needed to appear disconnected entirely. Several strategic meetings determined he must appear disconnected. It involved proxies and shifts in allegiances with some backstabbing. They said best for Jack to be seen as above it all if he was going to take over and steer everything in to a new, more profitable direction. There would be many quick demands for results and profit. They always wanted profit. Who wouldn't?

The sweat seeped over the lounge chair. Maybe a shower was in order. Then a quick check of the internet and cellphone. Not to communicate or anything, but have a little look. He couldn't though, but why not? He thrived on take overs and exploiting the weaknesses of others. Would he be better off in a village in Africa? At least he could do what he liked there. No, this beautiful beach had to suffice, but maybe he could take a car and go somewhere and do something. Why bother, all he wanted was to be back in New York ready to reclaim his throne. He paid his bill for the beach time and headed back to his hotel. Maybe he would go poolside. No, it was too much effort here for more profitable returns.

He dumped his stuff in his hotel room and noticed a message blinking on the landline. He listened and his heart sank.

He'd been duped, suckered, flimflammed, whatever one called it, he was fucked. He was broke. How could they have done it? It wasn't even his money. Or was it? He'd been leveraged to the hilt, but it was separate from his money, right? The ex-wife took a lot. Could it be that big a loss?

When you lose everything then yes.

How could he be so stupid?

He knew better and had been bested at his own lies.

Who could he trust? No one.

Connie maybe set the whole thing up for him to go away.

The Widow Parsons, the ex-wife, the son of Parsons, Parsons from beyond the grave.

It remained uncertain, but absolutely true.

He'd lost everything and there he was on vacation.

He couldn't even pay his bills.

It was all too fast. There's no way the banks already stopped his accounts. This was crazy.

No this couldn't be possible.

Were the goons playing a joke?

What could he do if he had no credit?

He needed to get back to New York immediately.

Who to call?

If Connie was in on it then no one.

He'd long lost most friends. The goons? Who could he trust to borrow money from?

He packed and lied to the clerk about returning. Then had to catch a bus to the station and switch for the cheap bus to San Jose.

Fucked, fucked, fucked, he thought, now you're in paradise. Why? Cause he had a renewed drive and vigor to get revenge and let heads be got. He only had to get back to New York. How hard could that be?

Rando if you don't know (III)

TO THE VICTIMS

Lately life gets one hoping that you aren't the victim because who is going to help you besides volunteers? Heroes are dead, they said.

MARLENE MURDERS

Bradley is finally going to get it for what he's done to me, Marlene thought. How could I have loved him for so long? I do love him still. Is this a good idea? Maybe he'll change. I feel so stupid for putting up with his shit all these years. God, I can't believe I was only nineteen when we met, and here I am, a wasted life at thirty-six. I sure was a sweet young thing back then. I didn't know no better, and he had those cowboy boots and Wranglers that showed off his butt. Now it's all fat and blubbery. I've seen it way too many times to see any joy in it. Seventeen fucking years with that asshole! I don't know why I didn't think of this sooner.

Not long after high school, I was out at some bar for underage drinkers in Lowdon, and he walks up all cock of the walk and chats me up good. He was the first man to ever pay attention to me. I was shy, and thanks to him I still am.

I want this. I need this freedom. I've got to do it. I can't look back on something that's not there. Or feel nostalgic about a man who beats me whenever he's mad; a man who sent me to the hospital three times in a month. I lied for him then. Well I ain't lying no more. The truth is that me killing him is probably the best thing. He's got to go for what he's done.

I thought maybe the baby would change things for us. Help us turn a corner. Get over our problems and move forward. My belief. My stupidity. I knew deep down it was the last thing he wanted to hear.

I thought he'd be happy. Maybe I chose the wrong time to tell him. No, as Doreen says, it's not my fault, damn it. That bastard is the only one to blame. An eye for an eye as the preacher used to say. Why did he have to go and punch me in the stomach when I told him?

I even said hit me in the head instead. He was so drunk he probably doesn't know what he done.

He'll be up soon 'cause he's been passed out for a while. If in I'm gonna do this, I'd better get on with it. He sure looks calm snoring away. Bastard. Why did he have to kill our baby? Get it over with, come on Marlene, hold yourself together. Take the knife. Steady now. Like the internet says, a cut to the jugular will do it. Plunge it. Hit the fucker!

God, why can't I do this? Don't cry. Don't be weak. I can't do it. Shit! Why am I so weak? I let him walk all over me. Am I going to let him get away with killing my baby too? Will I ever have a baby again? Life feels so cold. And it's his fault.

Or is it mine? I could have run. I could have left. But I stayed and I stayed. Even Mama thinks I'm a damn fool. Well I done proved her right. And what am I going to tell my family? They say never to tell anyone before the first trimester. I guess it was, what is it, bad karma? Or a curse? Am I cursed? What am I going to do when he wakes up?

He can't wake up. I'm a fool. I'd better put the knife

away and make him some coffee. He's going to need it if he's going to function today.

"Whatch you doin' there woman?" Bradley says.

Can I turn around and face him? One more time I have to hear that voice of the killer. The one who fucks around and doesn't give two shits about me. Thanks for the herpes. The one that hits me and calls me stupid and an ugly piece of shit. The one that took away my last hope for anything. No, I'm not going to be beat no longer. No, I ain't taking his shit no more. I've got to be fast. Come on, turn around and do it!

"Whoa," he says when he's lying there, and I hold the knife to his throat. "What'd I do this time now? You can't blame me if I don't remember, can you?"

Don't cry and don't show weakness or he'll grab the knife and beat me more. Hell no! Do it!

"You ain't getting out this one Bradley. You killed my baby and, and, and . . ."

Now! Ugh!

I plunged it in before he could say anything clever. A trickle turned to a stream of red.

Hold it in there.

He can't speak, and he can't save himself.

"How you like that? I ain't afraid of you no more."

And now take it out. There's that gurgling sound. Oh my God all that blood everywhere all over the room. All over me. It feels hot. It feels good. Ha ha ha! Oh joy. I feel, I feel, I feel like I am being purified. My sins are flushing away from me. It feels good. I'm going to be free soon.

I'll stay here a while and watch him die.

THE KLASH

The Klash is a fashion victim turned superhero. The Klash (k not c, so as to avoid copyright issues with the great eighties band) fights crime wearing a mish-mash of styles, colors, and patterns that confuses criminals.

Weapon of choice: the Klashnikov

Not to be confused with the AK47, the K fires rubber bullets that explode on targets' bodies with a set of industrial dyes of dazzling colors; all of which have never been animal tested and are strictly vegan. They temporarily render the criminals bedazzled.

Just in time for a quick fashionable cuffing and makeover before being handed over to the police, usually saying the catchphrase: "You'll look great for your court date."

ARE YOU AWARE OF CAPOEIRA?

Are you aware of Capoeira?
I'm aware a Capoeira.
I wear my cap while I do my Capoeira,
while I do my Capoeira.
Dancin' feet in the streets while I do my Capoeira.
Are you aware a Capoeira?
I'm aware of Capoeira.
I wear my cap while I do my Capoeira,
while I do my Capoeira.
Are you aware of Capoeira?
I'm aware a Capoeira.
I wear my cap while I do my Capoeira,
while I do my Capoeira.
Dance to defend myself and my friends.
It never ends!
Are you aware a Capoeira?
I'm aware of Capoeira.
I wear my cap while I do my Capoeira,
while I do my Capoeira.
Dance in the streets while I do my Capoeira,
while I do my Capoeira.
You a cap wearer Capoeira?

FIGHTER NOT A LOVER: CLIVE

Sixteen, young and dumb: Clive told the guy to pull the trigger.

To Clive's surprise, the guy did.

Deep pain followed.

Clive lost the tip of his finger to a bullet and his hand to infection.

Twenty-two, dumb still, Clive remained the type always looking to beef, escalate a tiff, eager for a slight, turn a fester into rage. He'd be there ready for a diss, a comment, a funny look, whatever, always prepared to fight a lost argument or take an opposing side.

Friends called him Stumpy. Some got a black eye for it. Soon any real friends thinned to only one miscreant named Daryl.

A black eye, Clive's specialty with the stump, knew no gender roles. The stump was equally destructive.

Some women were impressed, at least for a little while. Such rage to cage.

Clive ran from one "piece" to the next "piece" never looking back.

If a guys' look turned to whichever girl Clive claimed possession at the moment, no matter how fleeting, he'd rather fight the looker than fuck the woman, which was not the best way to work out one's aggressions carelessly.

He got off on the aggression. Some women got off on the attention, few got off with Clive.

Twenty-five, alone, Clive bled out by a gutting shot in a bar's back alley due to a dispute over the Chargers; a series of tussles tussled too far.

Nine years on from the shot off fingertip and lost hand, Clive never learned: Don't say pull the trigger. They might.

Rando if you don't know (IV)

READY?

"You ready for this good day?"

"You know it."

"All right, all right have a good one then."

"You too."

THE GOODBYE PARTY

Mark and Kelly said goodbye to the money and a displeased cat, Mr. Pepmore. Perhaps they decided to deny their recent woes and fate, or being near each other ignited feelings of safety.

Either way, they happily walked out the Union Square Hotel holding hands, occasionally skipping. They simply enjoyed each other's company.

Their carefree affection stopped while Kelly fished for her MetroCard, but otherwise bliss continued in the subway station and on the L out to the Graham stop in Williamsburg.

Above ground, Mark and Kelly affectionately sauntered along. They stopped off at a bodega realizing they needed to bring something.

Mark normally would have brought a six pack, and probably mooched a few more after finishing all six, but no alcohol meant no beer, so he bought a two liter of ginger ale.

Mark realized he didn't have a gift for Stacey. How could he not have a gift?

Kelly suggested a bouquet of carnations from the bodega.

Mark wasn't a flower guy, but they'd do.

They traversed the post-industrial streets of Williamsburg until reaching Stacey's apartment. An unknown purple haired woman came to the door, and gladly welcomed them in, noting most people hung back in the garden.

After pointing to a cooler for drinks, the greeter gave a disrespectful eye to the ginger ale.

Walking back Mark thought this disheveled mess of an apartment was a part of Stacey he barely knew. She had artsy type roommates that were her friends, but she never discussed them with him.

Mark and Kelly found the garden packed with probably fifty chattering guests. The grill sizzled in the background and the latest, greatest unknown band only listened to twice—once to say it was cool, twice for verification, then never again—played out the speakers.

Mark didn't know anyone, but tried to avoid appearing entirely lame at a party of younger hipsters with Kelly observing. They were still in the budding phase of their relationship, and he needed to impress.

He jumped into a conversation and soon brought Kelly into the mix. He contemplated Stacey's whereabouts.

Was it the right party?

Mark and Kelly continued their conversation with strangers mostly about New York real estate.

Somewhere in a room above a glass smashed and yelling ensued. The crowd of partiers slowly stopped talking and began to listen as the threatening shouts grew louder.

Mark thought he heard Stacey's voice and decided to investigate telling Kelly he'd be back.

Inside the apartment, he followed the shouts upstairs to a closed bedroom door.

Mark put his ear to the door. Voices screamed at each other. Mark heard Stacey's voice. He didn't know whether to intervene.

A bang and a crash inside the room caromed outward.

Mark opened the door.

Inside a hipster held a broken bottle to Stacey's throat, while a heavily tattooed woman stood near.

Who the hell are you? The hipster demanded.

Mark, Stacey screamed, go away!

Let her go, Mark said, and moved in closer to assess the situation.

The tattooed woman turned to block Mark, brandishing a knife. She had eyebrows tattooed where the hair should be and a small checkerboard on her right cheek.

Are you a cop? the tattooed woman asked.

Not exactly, Mark said.

He's cool, Stacey said.

First time Mark ever heard that from her.

This bitch isn't going anywhere until she pays us, the hipster said.

For what, Mark said.

Coke, what do you care, the tattooed woman said.

How much, Mark said.

$2000, the hipster said still holding the bottle on Stacey.

Stacey shook uncontrollably.

Mark looked at Stacey wondering about the coke habit, but stopped and turned to the hipster and tattooed woman.

I'll pay it, Mark said, I need a little time, but I can get you the money.

How much time, the hipster asked.

An hour tops, Mark said.

Mark this isn't your problem, it's mine, Stacey said.

I don't care, Mark said, I'll pay it to get these fuckers out of here.

We don't care either, the hipster said, if you want to pay, whatever, I don't give a fuck, I only want the money owed.

How much did you say? Mark asked.

Two grand, the tattooed woman said.

Fine, Mark said thinking quickly, wait here.

Mark headed outside to find a few others standing in the hallway looking on.

They asked Mark what was happening.

Mark said not to worry, to go back to the party, he had it under control. Or something far from it, he thought.

Mark went out back and found Kelly, saying, he couldn't explain, but he needed her to not ask questions and to urgently go back to the hotel, and get three thousand dollars from the bag and to return ASAP.

Kelly looked puzzled but agreed and soon left.

Mark returned to the room where Stacey was being held.

The money should be here in forty-five minutes, Mark said.

The party continued.

For those in the room, the time passed agonizingly slow.

The hipster was named Kip and the tattooed woman Dawn. They explained they'd only wanted what Stacey owed them after they had let her get away with several bullshit promises to pay them back. They heard she was leaving town, so they had to be rough and get the money or else.

Mark kept cool. He was angry at Stacey but didn't show it.

Why was she going the route of her sister?

Kip asked Mark why he cared.

Mark started to say she was like family, but instead said, don't ask.

But Mark asked Kip to take the bottle away from Stacey's neck suggesting she wouldn't go anywhere and if he hurt her then there would be no money. We can all wait here civilized like, right? he said.

Kip agreed, but said Stacey had better not move.

Dawn sheathed her knife in a further move of détente.

Time ground on.

Everyone mostly ignored each other's gazes and sat in uncomfortable silence.

Mark focused on an unplugged lamp shaped like a horse head.

Most other items were labeled in boxes: Bathroom, Bedroom, Desk, etc.

At least she is moving, Mark thought.

In record time, Kelly caught the L, rushed to the room, counted the money with Mr. Pepmore, and returned on the L, all in about forty minutes.

Kelly knocked on the door.

Mark answered and went outside to Kip's consternation, but said don't worry.

Record time, Mark said taking the money from Kelly saying don't speak, but go hide in the bathroom until I come get you.

Kelly left, disappointed at being relegated to the WC.

Mark carefully counted out the money and returned to the bedroom.

You got the money? Kip asked.

Yeah, count it, Mark said tossing Kip the money.

Kip counted and Dawn gazed as the bills passed through Kip's hands.

Mark picked up the horse lamp.

Kip finished counting and looked up saying it was one thousand over.

That's for your hospital bill, Mark said and cracked

the lamp over Kip's head. Then he punched Dawn hard in the jaw.

Dawn fell.

Mark kicked Kip in the ribs. He felt good taking out his frustrations, and thought to give a few more punts.

Mark soon stopped though telling Kip and Dawn to rethink their career choices, as they stumbled out.

Thank you, Stacey said hugging Mark.

We need to talk, Mark said.

I should explain, but my party, my friends, Stacey said.

I don't care, Mark said, you're coming with me, I've had the most ridiculous day and I can't deal with anything happening to you, and there's more going on than this, so we're going and besides there's someone I want you to meet.

Who, Stacey said.

Her name's Kelly, Mark said, as they entered the hallway. She's in the bathroom.

Mark knocked on the bathroom door.

Kelly answered and Mark told her all was clear, that they needed to go.

The two women smiled and shook hands.

Let's go, Mark insisted. We can catch up later.

I have to stay and say goodbye, Stacey said. It's my goodbye party.

Not now, Mark said raising his voice.

They fled the apartment.

When they reached the sidewalk, a voice in the shadows called out to Mark: Mr. McCann, we need to talk.

Not again, Mark thought, and told Stacey and Kelly to run!

JAKE THE CHATTING CAT

Jake is a catty cat
Best friend is a bat
Scourge is a rat
Occasionally likes to eat
Sometimes oats with notes of barley
Has been known to chew qat
Goes to a wat
Used to use the phrase homey don't play dat
Holds no claims to be fat
Never supported the GATT
Doesn't like wearing a hat
Exercises his lat(s)
Walks across the blue mat
Gives the dog a pat
Detests Matt the rat
On a radiator is where he sat
Of his mom he inked a tat
Doesn't like fake words like yat or smat.

HELP! MY SON GOT A FACIAL TATTOO!

An Unanswered Letter to Advice Columnist Sandra Maldonado of *Scarsdale Parent Quarterly*:

RE: Help! My son got a facial tattoo!

Dear Sandra,

My son Travis graduated high school last year, and we had high hopes for him. But so far, as a young man, despite the best efforts of my wife Peggy and me, Travis has been adrift. He skipped college, even though he finished in the top twenty of his class and was accepted to several good schools. We spent thousands on tutors. Every job he's had, mostly in the food service industry, lasts about two weeks. He's in a band called War Wolf. We encouraged his music and creative outlets, but honestly the songs are punk-pop drivel. How can the lives of a bunch of teenagers, afforded nearly every privilege and opportunity, be so sad?

Then there was Sanja. She sports many piercings and tattoos. She even had two diamond studs on her lower back. Why? I don't know. Sanja got Travis into tattoos. It started with a sleeve tattoo on his left arm based on a design of geometric shapes that Sanja, an 'artist,' created. I created that arm, dang it! Peggy and I weren't happy, but we decided like always that Travis should do what he wanted to do. I think we read the wrong parenting advice books when raising him. I recall one entitled: *Your Child is Super, Special, Fantastic and Don't Let Them Forget It*, or something like that. Maybe we should have disciplined him more? Maybe we should have instilled a stronger work ethic, instead of always cleaning up after him. Maybe we should have told him that when he gets older, he'll need to get a job.

At least the sleeve tattoo could be covered up by a long sleeve shirt. But his tattoos continued. Whatever little money he made, plus the allowance we gave him, went to more tattoos. He was a walking scab for several months. Every week a new tattoo appeared. Peggy almost fainted when the blood dripping fang marks appeared on his neck.

It was Sanja's influence. Sanja told Peggy that she loved the way Travis was out there, exposing his true self to the world. How original? Wasn't that what Warwolf was for? It was sexy, Sanja said. Sexy! I'm not exactly a prude. I grew up in the eighties and had my fair share of wild times, like trying a doobie in the *Miami Vice* days, but I got myself together and grew up when I had to, which was when Peggy told me she was pregnant. But I don't know if Travis ever can.

For whatever reason—it was young love after all— Sanja dumped Travis. He stewed way too much. And what did he do? Move on, think about his goals, his aspirations in life, his future, get a new girl? No, he got a facial tattoo!

It's an anchor, over an inch big, located below his left eye. It's so distracting, you can't escape it. I asked him what it meant. He said he didn't know; he didn't want to be cliché. Like having an anchor on your forearm was cliché, so somehow this broke all boundaries of art. This is my radical son. We offered to pay for laser removal. Travis said no. I told him he'd basically locked himself out of ever entering and becoming normal part of society. He's only nineteen for Chrissakes! Youth do stupid things all the time, I know, but this facial tattoo is ludicrous. Really that's how one has to be out there, separate from the crowd these days? I'm at a loss. Peggy's at a loss. I can't imagine how his grandparents will react at Thanksgiving: "What do you mean it won't come off? It's permanent? Pass the mashed potatoes, please!"

It's not our fault or is it? We thought we were good parents. Okay, we coddled him, gave him everything he wanted, and supported him with whatever he desired: soccer, karate, tennis, piano, summer camp, video games, fencing, biking, guitar. Guitar stuck, but nothing else. He dropped most interests within days of us buying the gear. Surely, he never did anything that was permanent before, why all those silly tattoos? We looked the other way when we found booze in his room at fifteen and weed at sixteen It was a phase Peggy said, and he was doing well at school. We'd done it all too. But c'mon a facial tattoo? We don't know what to say or do. Our precious boy's face has a darned anchor on it. We somehow failed as parents and that freaking tattoo reminds me every time I see Travis. It's so off-putting.

But what can we do? I can't imagine what he'll do the next time he wants attention.

Peggy and I decided to keep encouraging laser removal, and set up a savings account for Travis, solely for that purpose—the if-you-change-your-mind-fund. God, I hope he does. Peggy's even trying to stay positive about it somehow, and has been looking online for Tattoo Artist Schools, but apparently they don't exist. Travis said he is a canvas not a painter. Past payments to art instructors verify that. In our living room we still have a framed painting of Travis' of what was supposed to be a donkey from the eighth grade. It looks elephant-like. So, I am asking you, Sandra, what are we to do about the facial tattoo?

Sincerely,

Rod Childress, Esq.

Please note: Sandra does not consider queries for children above the age of eighteen.

URGENT CARE

"It's an emergency! Help! I have a splinter in my finger," the man said.

"Sir, having a splinter in your finger isn't an emergency," the 911 operator said.

"No, it's a big splinter and now it's an emergency, I pulled it out and there's blood."

"How much blood?"

"Gobs of blood are trickling over my finger."

"Sir, trickling is not an emergency. Basic first aid in your home should suffice. Are you near a sink? Do you have a bandage?"

"I don't know. I don't know. The blood is oozing."

"First, stop the bleeding. If you don't have any bandage handy, grab some toilet paper or paper towels and apply pressure to the wound."

"Okay, okay, oh gosh, hold on. I can do this."

"Yes, you can . . ."

"Okay, got it, the paper and the pressure."

"Good, hold it down tight for a long time."

"How long?"

"Maybe five minutes, then wait and see. That should stop the bleeding. Then clean the wound and place a bandage or even tape over it."

"You are a life saver."

BRUSHIN'

Brushin' like a Russian on the Fourth of July . . .
What? Is nothing special.
I do it every day.
Brush teeth.
Once. Twice. Three times daily.
Is good for you.
Floss too.
Maybe mouthwash.
Da.
Inside.
Outside.
Backside.
Front side.
Left side.
Right side.
Top side.
Bottom side.
Mezzanine!
Do the repeating.

THIS DIRTY OLD HOUSE

Construction took longer than expected. The contractors botched a few spots. I've still got an uneven foundation thanks to some inept worker from years ago. You have to look closely, but I know where it is. It gave me an inferiority complex when I was younger, but I've overcome that now that I'm one of the oldest houses on the block. I've made it through and seen a lot in eighty odd years, as in beyond my lot. If you passed by me, you might call me 2108. I prefer Dom as in domicile. I've always liked the ring of that word like my door bell.

Gus and Vera Gladstone paid to build me in 1952. They lived out their golden years using me as their abode. I'm a two-story with four windows in the front (twenty altogether). I've got a full-sized basement and a nice porch for rocking. I'm strong, made of redwood, that's where I stand out from the rest of the block. Paltry pine wasn't good enough for the Gladstones. My ancestors came from the great forests of northern California.

Those were the days when I was a fresh young house on the block. I hooked up with foxy little hoes all over the neighborhood. Basically, if you are two stories, or more you are a male house, and if you are one story you are a female house. At least where I come from. No one knows what to make of the A-frames, not that there's anything wrong with them, but, in general, we let them keep to themselves.

My only real competition was Brickhouse. This ornery old man of a house who likes to gloat about how indestructible he is because he's made of brick. The girly houses liked him because he was strong and fireproof. A real bad boy, but he never grew flowers like me. Oh, I guess Brickhouse isn't that bad all in all, but he's still dumb as a rock.

One of my best times was when I hooked up with this cute little house down the street. She was a saucy spruce. She enjoyed letting me enter through the back door. It always felt good, like you were a special guest. She had a nice pair of dormers back then. But she's been done over so many times she doesn't look the same. Her latest expansion project included a gaudy Florida room on the side and double-glazing on the front. She looks bloated, if you ask me. She changed from a hothouse to a derelict frame of her former self. She's let herself go with all that ivy creeping up her sides. I guess I'm sagging too.

Then there was that one time I got it on with that ho down the street made of cherry. She was the hottest thing on the block. Brickhouse and I competed to see who would get to her first. I got one over on Brickhouse and popped that cherry. Open house is what it was. She was probably too young for me, but like they say if there's moss on the shingle then let's mingle. Don't get me wrong, she was of age, certified hardwood, and legal. They had just sodded her lawn as if she needed it. Man, she was smoking that night and it wasn't her fireplace. We experienced a night of passion. We were knocking boards. The block shook mightily. But we had nothing in common. Cherry and redwood don't go together.

The aftermath proved too much for me. I couldn't stand to listen to her groaning. Then the little garage came that she claimed was mine. I believed her until I discovered the garage was made of pine. It was one of the other houses on the street who had to deal with that nightmare. Cherry was cute until they tarted her up too much with peach shutters and a big green door that invited anyone in. I entered first, but then she let everyone from the district in her front door. Poor little garage.

The Gladstones died and their offspring didn't care to keep me. I got a lot of dirty looks when the next family moved in. They treated me well, and I had no reason to discriminate. These were the Jenkins, an African American family. They were the first black family on the block and caused a lot of controversy. There were hyped up cries of lost property values. I didn't feel any cheaper. Hell, they were fun. I was still made of redwood. Soon though the white flight happened, and I was smack dab in the middle of a bustling African-American neighborhood. I was the Jenkins' first home, and they took care of me.

Despite a few dings and nasty gash on my side from a 4th of July accident, the kids behaved, but then they grew up and went to college. First in the family. I was proud since I'd helped raise them. But they never came back except for the odd holiday. Mr. Jenkins died of sickle cell anemia. Mrs. Jenkins spent her last years alone with me. She had a modest pension, and couldn't afford to maintain me.

More and more leaks punctured my roof. My paint chipped and my foundation sagged. I felt miserable and things only got worse. I liked Mrs. Jenkins and it was a shame to have to watch her deteriorate. The kids barely visited. As soon as Mrs. Jenkins died of old age, the kids tried to sell me, but there were no takers. The neighborhood had gone downhill thanks to crack and meth. I was virtually abandoned.

It got so bad that when strong winds blew, I feared I might collapse. Even old Brickhouse felt sorry for me, I think. I was in a horrible state.

Crackheads started using me as a hang out to get high. Someone took a shit on my floor. Who does that? Savages.

After several shoddy years some venture capitalist, who had seen an infomercial about making money by fixing up cheap property and renting it out, came along.

The VC made superficial repairs neglecting my ailing foundation. I turned out new tenants unhappy with my poor wiring, busted pipes and drafty chill about every six months for quite some time.

For a while I was a party house for some artists. Those were decadent times for me.

Sadly, they didn't have many ideas besides how to get stoned and fuck each other. So, they starved or moved back to the places from which they came.

I lost a good neighbor, Woody, when some punks set him on fire one Halloween.

Halloween is probably one the worst days for houses. You run the risk of getting egged, having toilet paper streamed all over your front yard, or worse.

Christmas is bad in a different way. I hated it when the tenants decked me out with a bunch of tacky lights and threw Rudolph next to the Baby Jesus in my front yard.

After some time, things turned around.

Gentrification came thanks to slumming yuppies looking to turn a profit with real estate speculation. These yuppies were the DINS (Dual Income, No Sex) types and rather boring. Seriously boring. Maybe the yuppies used me like a cheap shack, but it felt nice to be taken care of again by people.

They cleaned my yard and gave me a big deck. Brick-house was jealous, and I was back in business with the single stories.

Middle class families with kids followed the yuppies and they cleaned up the neighborhood.

The Millers moved into me. We started to have neighborhood picnics. Houses swapped pies with each other during the holidays.

I heard the return of families had to do with location of the new mall built with many amenities at the old glass factory site where many of the original neighbor people used to work.

Apparently, my neighborhood had lacked shopping for a spell.

The Millers changed me in a positive way. They put aluminum siding all over me.

I was ashamed at first because the siding hid my true Redwood roots. I got used to it though. I felt restored.

They did a lot on my insides too, and even replaced my septic tank. Maybe they had to, I'd gotten some unexplained odors.

With the siding I don't worry about the wind anymore. It's way warmer, and I'm the best-looking house on the block again.

All you have to do is power wash me and I'm clean.

Next to Brickhouse, I look great because he's started to get chips in his brickwork.

He grumbles more than ever, especially since I knock on a lot more doors than he does.

HEART ATTACK SNACKS HEIR

Helen struggled over what to do with the legacy of her parents' food products empire, Porker, which nearly everyone enjoyed in the Heartland, with favorites like:

- Bacon sticks: ya know like fish sticks but with bacon.
- Cheesesteak cake: Provolone-based cheesecake with chopped steak, onions and peppers baked in (Add Whiz for an extra 50¢ in Philly).
- Fried cheddar jalepeño potato balls with ranch.

But diets and tastes changed.
Helen wanted to take the business vegan.
The Board said no.
That fatal decision meant Porker no more.

CARNIE BOOK

Carnie Lore: Portraits from my year of dangerous fun on the edge of society

Writer Brett Stetwick gets famous for writing *Carnie Lore,* which he claims to be non-fiction. Turns out the memoir is based on a lie that gets bigger:

The penultimate knife fight described in Brett's book never happened.

Carnie love and their rituals he described, like drinking pig's urine before sex, are a sham.

Brett never operated the pony rides or the water rifles.

No one ever fucked him for a giant pink panda.

He never witnessed a fellow carnie spitting on hot dogs to add salt, nor another greasing up a pig for a special orgy helmed by the ringleader to bring the performers closer together.

Brett's first promotional radio show interview starts off with the back story about a small Oregon town and longing for adventure and a fated night when he asked for extra butter on his popcorn, never looking back.

A call-in caller calls out the lies.

Little people knife throwers in Elvis masks: TCB.

Take Care of Business?

No, Take Care of Brett the next night.

With Brett dead, the book tour ends, but the book sells well.

Eventually, the success leads to a movie produced by Brett's estate: *Carnivore: The Reckoning*

Real carnies eat Brett.

Most book proceeds go to the estate's trustee, Brett's half-sister he never met, Elaine.

Rando if you don't know (V)

AN OBJECT

Definitely not something smaller than before, but nothing you want to see or feel or hear or taste or smell? It's awful. The smell, if only you smelled it, then you'd know.

THE EXCHANGE

At a time between when the Berlin Wall fell (1989) and when Germany reunited (1990), and when The Scorpions' *Wind of Change* was popular, Dirk, a German exchange student, arrives in a small midwestern U.S. town called Hamburg. Dirk soon ruins the gig of the German language teacher, Mr. Schmidt.

Largely speaking a made-up language of his own, Schmidt doesn't *sprechen sie deutsche* so *gut,* and lied to students and ignorant faculty for years.

Funny at first when Dirk calls out Schmidt's misunderstanding of having fire. Schmidt then claims he's teaching in a Swiss German dialect. Dirk says he has relatives in Zurich.

The story turns *schwarz* with Schmidt plotting to kill Dirk to save his career and pension.

Being an East German, Dirk is too innocent to know better, and lets in a killer pretending to be a vacuum salesman. But the supposed salesman is too coked up to accurately stab Dirk.

Dirk's exchange family mother, Doreen, steps in and whacks the salesman on the head with a hammer.

The salesman confesses to police that Schmidt paid him, and the town finds itself wrapped up in its biggest scandal since the lynching of a carnie in the 1970s.

Speculation, *er sagte, er sagte* ensue in court.

But the vacuum salesman's confession dramatically recounted by the D.A. seals Schmidt's fate in the jury's eyes. *Schuldig.*

Former students stand with Schmidt picketing for leniency after the verdict. But no one understands their gibberish German. *Ich verstehe nicht,* Dirk said nearly every day of his exchange.

Dirk left for Germany confused having not improved his English as much as he'd hoped.

Upon return to the Fatherland, he told his girlfriend, I cannot find this story amusing . . .

Rando if you don't know (VI)

FIGHTIN' WORDS

Fightin' words, that's what you heard.
If I survive tonight, then we'll be all right.
But words are proud, and we'll say them loud.
They're fightin' words, that's why you hurt.

JUST JAY

Red Jay
Blue Jay
Black Jay
Grey Jay
White Jay
Pink Jay
Yellow Jay
Green Jay
Orange Jay
Brown Jay
Purple Jay
Steller's Jay
No way!
Just Jay (Rainbow version)
And that's a-okay.

DRUM CIRCLE

Taking a seat with smiles all around the circle, Reginald felt the rhythms hit his body. Thunderous beats faster and faster.

Reginald tried to get in sync with the vibe of the drum circle, but he couldn't keep the beat, and remained two beats behind from everyone else's, and then three and more.

The initially welcoming looks of mostly dreadlocked men of African descent soured.

Reginald's taps kept swinging to a different beat, most might say with no rhythm, definitely no percussive persuasion. There was no specific rhythm required per se, just a clear sound for all.

A certain uniformity and syncopation usually took place.

It didn't help that Reginald wore a baby blue duck suit with questionable support stockings of chartreuse, and a T-shirt hinting at being the upper point of a swastika, but maybe it was misconstrued.

To the others it was for love and the bongo.

For some dreamscape in Reginald's mind, it was for money. That is if he could learn to play.

The men of the drum circle would be the best to learn from, but undivided observation wasn't Reginald's specialty. He needed to be into it, and the moments wherever he could tap in, he took them. If that meant out of rhythm beats, that was that to him. But alas not the rest.

Eventually, a bearded black man with greying dreads approached Reginald giving a signal to stop.

Reginald obliged and then the man said it's a slow build UC, and began tapping his drum at a steady back and forth. The one and then the other and back and around, and he suggested Reginald follow.

Reginald paid attention, and the rhythmic song of the sunny Sunday continued unabated, despite the duck man's efforts to snort it inadvertently with too much pizzazz.

The impromptu band played on, and Reginald melted in.

Rando if you don't know (VI.5)

STARRING

What if the universe is expanding because when you die, or anyone or anything dies, they become a star?

DISCOMBOBULATED

Tired, I get home, unlock the door. Turn on the lights. A murderous row of five freaks await me ready to rumble. Turn off the lights knowing I have a split second to hit the goon on the right with a jab, flip round to kick the bits of the center bat-bearing oaf. Skull punch the far right freak and gouge the eyes of his neighbor center right, then back over to the left kick, punch, uppercut . . . he's out and back to the beginning reach for that ear. Pull. Smack nose up into brain. Back to center. Smash, kick, and twist the neck until dead. Three left. Back to right round-house to the conservative side, and clutch and yank that neighbor's throat out. Two left. Pull their heads together: crunch. Discombobulated. Again, for two more rings. Turn on the lights see what's left. They hobble. No mercy. Smash the temple right hard and round over to trip, then bang the neck on the floor crushed. One more. Weave and wobble. Mother-fuckers in my house can't touch me! Grab the leg, animal wrench his ankle. Feel it crack left. Broken. Stomp twice. Double check. No breath in them but I am steaming and heaving deep. Reset and stretch. Turn off the lights. Now what?

PAPA'S AFTERNOON

A bar called Papa's sat on the edge of an industrial heap far removed from the good company of downtown. A small cinder block building focused on spirits and minimalism, it provided air conditioning to relieve the steamy afternoon for a few men looking for hope and courage in a glass, including Horace.

Following another row, Horace escaped his miserable domestic situation pondering his point of return to Belinda. Her words were so hurtful and his actions spiteful.

What was the point of going on? Would they end it after so much co-dependency? After six years of love, hate, and rage? There'd been lots of rage, and physical abuse to go with the mental from both sides. But they'd hold on.

Was it for Cameron their two-year-old? Maybe. Was it convenience? Maybe. Was it love? Yes, their love still existed, though spit and stepped on every which way.

A few years ago, Horace would have gone to a place like Papa's looking for a fight, but he'd lost his edge. If he'd admit it, he came in the afternoons more often than prime time to avoid the young bucks. He had Cam to think about, and no boy should respect a beat man. That's what his daddy taught him.

Horace ordered another rye on the rocks.

MURRAY IN PORTO

The line ceased. Murray worried why. He was ten people deep from Passport Control.

Be casual, he thought. He tried some of the subtle calming techniques he'd learned like curling his toes and deep breathing through the belly. He didn't want to lie, but must.

Get in and come back after the drop, they'd said. Do that and everything goes back to normal. Get through is the only objective, they said. Do it, they said, or your family dies.

The line moved and soon Murray stood by the yellow line: instructed to wait. Next a mustachioed customs control agent with a permanent scowl motioned Murray forward, asking for his passport. To that point, Murray hid his passport so as not to draw attention to his American nationality, not that it mattered in Portugal. They had tourists over from the U.S. all the time.

Hello, Murray said.

The customs official grunted, and flipped through Murray's passport.

Murray thought not too many stamps to cause suspicion.

The official swiped it through the reader, looked at the screen, looked at the passport, looked at Murray, and then excused himself from his booth.

Murray asked if there was a problem.

The official squinted his eyes and nodded, but Murray couldn't tell if it meant no or yes, or more likely shut up and wait.

Murray looked around and then turned to see the many faces of others queuing. He was holding them up. They knew something was wrong. He started to fret, but maintained his breathing. 1-4 in, 1-4 hold, 1-4 out, repeat.

The official came back, gave a slight grin and stamped Murray's passport.

The breathing worked, Murray thought, collecting his passport and walking to the baggage claim.

This is where it might get tricky, he thought. A customs guard walked by with a heavily panting German Shepard.

Murray thought the dog might pick up the scent, but the dog and guard moved on.

They'd instructed him to take his bag marked with a yellow sticker. The bag, if he got through, was to be picked up by a driver.

Murray milled about with the other TAP flight 214 passengers waiting for the conveyer belt to crank up and distribute bags.

He anxiously vied for a spot near where the bags came out.

About fifty bags landed on the conveyor before Murray's old brown leather suitcase with the yellow sticker trundled on. He grabbed it.

Now was the big moment. He had nothing to declare, just documents capable of destroying the world, bound for the wrong hands. How far must he fall?

His family would be free, if he delivered, they'd said. Murray had to believe them. He had no choice. His wife and kids might be dead already, he thought, but tried to stay positive. He cleared customs with no issue. Surprised, he'd almost wished they'd stopped him to stop everything.

A driver with a sign reading Palmero waited.

Murray considered, but then noticed a burley man near the driver. So he approached the driver, saying he was Palmero asking if he could get a good Port in Porto.

As planned, the driver said there was no time, *senhor.*

Rando if you don't know (VII)

PUSH BACK

Sitting with friends on a sidewalk, including a young man whom a young woman called "sweet" before leaving. Thinking that's a death sentence for the heart, whether he realizes it or not. The sun rose.

OUTSIDE THE LAB

0. They fucked the planet and themselves in how long?

1. About 200 seconds, sir.

0. Is this a joke?

1. No, sir.

0. How stupid could they be?

1. Stupidity isn't the issue, I mean they are stupid, but they are also incredibly selfish, evil, and most of all greedy. They used all the water first.

0. How's that even possible? Most of the planet and they are water.

1. Looks like they liked oil-made plastics and generally squandered everything.

0. What about the gold?

1. Used for economics.

0. What? Fuck that's stupid. Seafood?

1. Decimated.

0. Trees?

1. Wiped out.

0. The moon?

1. They contended it harnessed the tides and little more.

0. What a waste. Lava?

1. Never could get a handle on that.

0. Fuck, it was obvious.

1. Not to them. They mainly focused on procreating

and killing each other. They completely neglected their surroundings except a few. Collectively, they never saw themselves as stewards of the planet or it would seem appreciated the raw power of nature beyond figuring out trifling ways to exploit it.

0. And the sun?

1. They never figured it out.

0. Everyone could see it all damn day, how much more obvious could we be?

1. That flummoxed me too.

0. Surely, the wind?

1. For moving on water and some energy, but little else.

0. Squanderers and wasters. Even those dumbass dinosaurs made it to the end of the experiment.

1. I take full responsibility, sir.

0. No, my fault too. So much for new ideas on intelligent beings. This sets us back.

1. I say good riddance, sir.

0. Let's reset the planet. Go back to basics and try something new in the next cycle. What survived of interest?

1. Ferns, crocodiles, and cockroaches.

0. That's a start. Try again, and this time nothing walks on two legs. Keep the brains, but modify them to increase empathy and decrease pathos.

1. Yes sir, that could work.

0. It better or else we'll lose funding and have to blow it up for good.

SUCCUBUS

Peter Sanderson awoke feeling exhilarated nearing climax thinking how great his girlfriend Kate was. Opening his eyes, he gazed in absolute horror realizing a shrieking succubus, not Kate, straddled him and got him off. The figure appeared a sinister blend of demon and woman with a tormenting head reminiscent of a griffin. Peter tried to pull out and flee, but alas the succubus with its demonic shrieks and callous eyes would not be denied its pleasure.

Peter grew paralyzed and grimaced in ecstatic agony wishing he could turnover and push his head into a pillow to muffle the pain. The succubus rode Peter hard. Peter feared certain death as his level of suffering heightened every time the succubus gyrated.

Just when Peter felt his last breath near, the succubus climaxed letting out an exuberant, animal howl and explosion of liquid all over Peter. In a carnal poof, the succubus disappeared and Peter could finally move.

Seeing Kate lying next to him, he tried to stir her, but she would not wake.

A sticky liquid covered Peter, and began to harden like wax across his torso and creep over his body. Scared and frantic, he leapt out of bed and ran to the bathroom.

A near cast over his entire body formed by the time Peter stepped under a pouring showerhead. He quickly scrubbed himself fighting off the stiffening wax. His fight felt futile until he began punching desperately at his stomach where the thickest bit of wax solidified.

Following several bone-crushing blows, Peter managed to crack the core of the wax, which suddenly crumbled and collapsed onto the tub's floor. With the apparent core extracted, Peter peeled off the remainder across his body.

Peter's naked body heaved from scared, nervous inhales. He neared hyperventilation before slowing to steadier breaths. He started to inspect his body. Everything appeared intact, but several red welts peppered his stomach.

Distracted, Peter didn't notice the wax reforming around his feet. Suddenly the wax hardened again, and Peter, at the pure mercy of the menacing wax, lost his balance crashing hard taking the shower curtain and rod with him.

Writhing in pain, Peter had no time to see where the newly spilt blood on the floor originated. The creeping, stiffening wax ascending his legs proved a greater concern. Uncertain as to how to stop the wax, Peter put his hands below his knees as the wax approached. He let the wax take hold of his arms. When he felt a certain attachment to the wax, he ripped his arms off his legs and flung himself towards the toilet.

Peter's actions freed his legs because his motions caused the wax on his legs to stop solidifying. The wax on his arms and hands became his immediate new concern. He bru-tally banged his arms against the inner bowl of the toilet slowly cracking the wax. The harsh pounding against the porcelain caused the wax to break from his arms and fall mostly into the toilet.

Peter flushed the toilet as fast as possible. The bulk of the wax swirled down. He turned to see the remaining pieces of wax start to re-form on the floor and in the shower and rush towards him. Knowing that the remaining wax would put up a fight, Peter scooped up the bits from the floor and tossed them into the toilet and flushed once more. Then he turned on the hot water for the shower to temporarily stymie the leftover wax in the tub. The hot water steamed and forced the wax to slowly melt into the tub's drain.

Peter backed away wondering what was going on. Running his fingers through his hair, he noticed a strange slickness. He inspected his hand and reeled backwards at the sight of blood.

Peter yelled to Kate for help, but received no response. He turned to look in the mirror. His heart raced seeing his bangy brown hair soaked in blood. Worse still, he'd somehow neglected to notice that his face had been covered in wax save his eyes, mouth and nose. The thick wax formed a smooth shapely mask akin to a glow-in-the-dark skull. Peter instantly began punching his face; striking blow after blow until the wax crumbled, freeing his face from captivity. Despite, the blows, Peter's face remained free of noticeable wounds. His dull green eyes looked unusually lucid and horrified as if the greens of his eyes fought restlessly to stay encircled leaving a trail of blood shoots over the white surfaces to the crevices leading to his eyelids. Bags drooped under his eyes towards his slightly bent nose leading to his puffy lips and strong stubbly chin. In the other direction worry lines sunk deep into his forehead that usually lay behind his bangs, which stayed overhead matted in blood.

Taking a calming breath, Peter inspected his bruised body in the mirror and wondered what had happened. Did he battle hot wax after being fucked by some she-demon?

A trembling rumble came from the toilet. Peter stepped back from the mirror while the toilet shook violently. It looked as if the toilet would crack up from the tiled floor, but then the shaking stopped.

Curiously Peter leaned over the toilet to inspect.

Instantly, a solid slab of wax shot forth from the toilet smacking Peter in the face. The force sent Peter high against the wall before he fell and crushed the flimsy magazine rack below. The wax fell back into the toilet and somehow flushed itself.

Peter's jaw ached. He put his hand to his face feeling a large break in his jaw-line left of his chin. Blood squished around in his mouth and his jaw locked from the force of the blow. He screamed in muffled agony, but he could not open his mouth. It felt as though his lower teeth had pulverized his canines and smashed into his upper gums. He slunk down onto the floor uncertain as to what might happen next.

After several frightful moments, he collected himself as best he could. He tried to exit the bathroom but slipped on the blood-slicked tile floor. He fell hard on his knees and hands. The quick jarring motions shook his broken jaw violently, and a new piecing pain surged with no chance for a cry of relief since his mouth remained fixed. Blood filled his mouth and he thought he'd drown in his blood as the small trickle escaping his mouth was not enough to expel the blood gush flowing inside. Feeling he'd choke, he gasped for air.

Fighting off excruciating pain, Peter forced the blood-flow up through the holes in the roof of his mouth and out his nostrils. This created a continuous oozing of blood out his nose. He breathed through the small opening left in his mouth and out his nose with the blood. It wasn't enough and his body grew weak from a lack of oxygen.

In a rash moment, Peter decided he had to create a bigger opening. He slowly filed his fingers into his mouth and then pried his jaw ajar causing a new level of intense pain. Tears of blood streamed from his eyes and his mouth hung agape. His jaw felt entirely unhinged.

Everywhere he turned, Peter saw blood flowing freely from his mouth down his chest to the floor. At least he breathed, but then a new weakness from a loss of blood slowed his flight from the bathroom to a weak crawl on all fours into the bedroom.

Blood poured over the white carpet, as Peter crawled back towards the bed where Kate lay fast asleep. How had Kate slept through everything? When he reached her he pulled the covers from her body in an effort to wake her. Kate did not stir.

Peter shook her to no response. He checked for a pulse and a breath. The vital signs ceased, and Kate looked deadly still.

Peter freaked and attempted in vain to yell out any form of sensible speech. Instead his mumbles only zapped at his lowering energy. Kate remained motionless.

Peter reached for the phone on the nightstand. There was no dial tone, not even a busy signal. Peter gave up and struggled to get into bed next to Kate. He held her close. He lay helpless clinging to her limp body. Tears developed anew and Peter let the curdling blood well up in his mouth until it sealed off his breathing passages. He faded into darkness pondering a swing set he enjoyed in his youth.

HANK HOPE

A triangular mountain top rose in the distant horizon as the boat bobbed up and down. Trouble lay behind and the unknown ahead. Rumors of gold and savages said trouble may continue. On the boat, Sal readied the gear, while Hank managed the helm and the difficult intonations of Ms. Pettigrew, who they'd picked up waylaid a few hundred nautical miles back promising reward for taking her directly to Zanzibar. But the problem was Hank and Sal had obligations of a life or death nature that required immediate attention. Feeling captive, Ms. Pettigrew's protests grew stronger, louder, and tinged with acidic superiority.

From what Hank gathered, she was an educated woman and the daughter of someone important, but not rich enough to be on a bigger, more secure boat with many servants the way most well-off persons should be in these dangerous seas. That'd explain how they found her and the unconscious man she called Frank floating in the sea on remnants of a medium sized ship left over from an attack Ms. Pettigrew couldn't or wouldn't recall to Hank. Frank breathed. Maybe Ms. Pettigrew didn't realize the lengths Hank and Sal had gone to rescue her and how far behind it put them in their own circumstances when time was critical.

Initially, Hank figured they could make up time in the calming sea and that, if they had no other hiccups, they'd be in port only one hour behind. If he hired an extra man or two from the dock then they'd be close to all right and hopefully not annoy Boss too much. But then that was to rescue a damsel, not a damsel and her baggage, a limp, unconscious heavy man.

Or maybe she knew the sacrifices they'd made, but didn't give a shit. Either way, Hank decided to huddle with Sal on whether or not to toss her and the unconscious man back to sea. With or without life vests, depended on Ms. Pettigrew's next statement.

Rando if you don't know (VIII)

FAST LANE

For a faster life: make more phone calls.

HACKS FOR NOTHING

The real hack was to pick up Jimmy and Carl at 8:3opm, and drive them directly to Flatbush and St. Marks: no questions. Just drive. But the hack they thought was the real hack wasn't the real hack at all, but a different hack.

The traffic in Manhattan agitated Carl, and being a native he questioned the hack's decision to take the Brooklyn Bridge versus the Manhattan.

Surely the hack knew the Manhattan Bridge would dump them on Flatbush. Was the hack gaming them for a bigger fare? They were stuck and late.

Jimmy said they should have gone with Dominic in the livery cab, their usual ride.

But then the idea was to somehow blend in more in a yellow cab. Wasn't a black town car just as ubiquitous?

Plus, Dominic's black sedan was in the shop and possibly known to certain adversaries, so better to go with the random yellow.

Ahmad, the hack, was from Lebanon and in the midst of a serious discussion with his wife back in Beirut as to why their thirteen-year-old son was not doing so well at math. Surely, the boy knew math was fundamental to the computer programming degree he should be focusing on, even if university was five years away.

That conversation had led Ahmad to miss a turn to take a right onto Houston when looking for a fare. He had to stick on Broadway and ended up by two men looking for an old-fashioned fare. He'd wanted to get the FDR to Midtown for one more fare maybe and then head home to Astoria. Anywhere but Brooklyn.

Carl and Jimmy insisted on putting a large box that smelled funny in the middle of the back seat, instead of the trunk. The smell wreaked, even with the windows open. Ahmad carried on with his wife. Jimmy and Carl fumed in silence. It had been a long day. They needed to get back to Brooklyn. They were men of action. They would be late. Very late for the drop. They couldn't be late. They jumped out of the cab with the big box and said fuck you to Ahmad without paying and started carrying the box down the bridge.

Ahmad yelled, but didn't want to do much.

Ahmad was stuck and stiffed. He suggested his wife seek out a tutor recommendation from his friend Jamal.

Jimmy and Carl got a text they were too late. They threw the box over the bridge with a signal knowing sometime soon they'd have to go trawling. They needed a cab back to Manhattan.

Ahmad was available.

BAR CARTER

"Like all children, your child is special. But here's the thing, he's not that bright. He is a daydreamer. One day maybe some of his dreams will come out, but in mathematics he is a failure. He can barely remember the Pythagorean Theorem, despite ample tutoring. Therefore, I have no choice but to flunk him. And now take your entitled white lily ass and go fuck yourself."

"Ha! That's hilarious," one of the other drunken teachers told Ursula over the increasing crowds.

They were three drinks deep at McFadden's happy hour airing out the past week's tough times with students, parents, assistants, and the principals to name a few, plus the administrator of Carter Middle School. It was a ritual for some, a lovely place of friendship before feeding the cats and curling up to a good book.

For the waitress, it was a gathering of cheap tippers, except the one lady who made it up.

For the bartender it was the first big party of the Friday shift that involved a lot of margaritas and mimosas. Later it would be beer and whiskeys.

The teachers always finished by 8pm, but they'd been up since 6am, if not before.

STEEP MISERY

The cup of green tea still steeped when Dean decided to sip. Too soon, he thought. It was still too hot and bland. But he was nervous and needed something to do. He waited for his girlfriend Jane. She had some explaining to do. Dean didn't know if they could still call themselves boyfriend and girlfriend.

What with the lies and affairs and general sense of misery. But they had little Stuart. Dean calculated it would be cheaper to stay together. He expected lawyers and child support would be expensive. Even if the mother cheated and committed credit card fraud, but didn't they always reward custody to the mother?

Dean's friends and family said it was time to move on from Jane. But Dean couldn't and wouldn't. He believed in the relationship. He still loved Jane, even if she despised him. Was he a sucker? Maybe.

Desperate? Perhaps.

Scarred by his childhood, and unable to get out of a bad relationship? Yes, yes, and yes again. Jane wasn't coming. Dean sipped the tea. It was his third cup. He'd been waiting for more than an hour. He needed to pee, but he held out for Jane.

CURSIVE

The print originated from 1783—the year the American Revolution ended and George Washington said farewell to his officers at Fraunces Tavern in New York in December.

Made post haste, the print shows some of the officers standing as George gives a cheer.

With a print run of 200, today it is estimated that only about twenty-five prints survive.

They are the rare print that captured in real time, at least as close as possible back then, an image of a Founding Father with a drink in hand.

The history of the print that came into possession of the Museum of American Patriots (MOAP) is varied.

Housed for fifty years or more in a tavern in Brooklyn owned by a former soldier in Washington's Continental Army James Marshall Irving. He owned the Boerum Arms on Bond Street until it burned down in Irving's old age of seventy-two.

The print would have burned too, if Irving's grandson had not rescued it before the building's collapse.

And this is when the curse of the print many say began because the grandson Thomas Fitzroy Irving, something of a *ne'er do well,* saved the print instead of the two drunks passed out at the end of the bar. The grandson died from smoke inhalation.

The Irvings were never the same, but they had their print, which hung above various Irving mantles until purchased at a Queens flea market by an astute MOAP curator, or so he'd say.

Rando if you don't know (IX)

THE FOOT PALM READER
Gazing into the soles of your soul.

MARBLE MOUNT

Drive up to the Marble Mount house to see a body double that never turns toward you walking English wolfhounds. Must be a family reunion, including strange children. Older ones, teenagers, but they need to be cared for. A strange lost French couple living in the house are related. Big awkward meal and night. Then bodies of body doubles start turning up. The house is threatened. What to do with the bodies that have been sullied by the big dogs? Can't call the authorities. Must protect the house and the children. By the agreement of the whole family, the bodies of the body doubles must be removed.

Don't forget you found the Venus di Milo on the street last night after a horrible date and rough job interview.

Rando if you don't know (IX.5)

JACKALS
Smack! The black-backed jackal pack attacked a yak for a tasty snack.

OLDER SOULS

Some cultures believe that when someone dies another person is born with that person's traits and personality being passed over the other side of the world. Although there is not quite full recognition or similarity in these rebirths. And these rebirths do not happen every time. New derivatives of the human experience are born as humanity evolves and the population grows. Rather these people's traits are reborn, but different or referred to as the old souls.

Those people that you somehow know have a little more depth and understanding and perspective on things compared to those only born once. And this doesn't necessarily refer to those deemed 'born again' by religious types. The problem with the old soul is they are best avoided in some instances.

This is often connected to how the old soul passed away from their previous life. For instance, getting hit by a bus when you are trying to get home to get laid and it was a sure thing, might put your old soul in a permanent bad state. Yet the new body that the old soul occupies may never know why they just might be perpetually miserable. But no one was ever always that way.

Peel back the fruit and there is usually something sweet and juicy inside. It's a matter of whether they turned rotten at some point. On the other end, you have the old souls who passed peacefully surrounded by loved ones and probably dying in their sleep. They reached nirvana and eclipsed this life for something more universal and heavenly, but remnants of their old soul still get passed on as an example of success in to a new body.

This too has been happening since the dawn of humanity. But when you see one of the remnants of one that made it, you might think that this person is permanently high or missing something. And that's because they are. These people tend to be overly joyful with a perma-grin without clear explanation or drug abuse. Many people do not understand them and they often end up as worshippers in spiritual retreats, ashrams, and on occasion cults, generally content with the simple joys of life. This often pisses off, or leads to misunderstandings, with the newer souls.

You have to comprehend the blissfuls and many different personalities of old souls across the spectrum, with new traits etching out in slightly different variables of new souls all the time. It's a constant expansion of humanity that may be on the edge of collapse, some say.

How many more variables can you have? Some might ask. Others believe its infinite and the soul business will go on in perpetuity.

We may never know, despite our best efforts at a proper soul search. Simply expressing these ideas are dangerous. Do depart this earth yet, lest they catch you.

AN ABHORRENT ARBORIST

The arborist kept a dirty secret to stay in business. To get repeat customers, he'd developed a clear toxic mix to place on a prized tree in a client's yard. The mix wouldn't kill the tree immediately. It started with limbs here and there, "something to watch," before being declared rotten.

Eventually after several years of limb trimming and chipping, the arborist could advise the client that, well, with all the limbs gone and the core clearly rotten that tree had to come down. That the stump was best removed and replaced with a fresh new tree. The arborist recommended a Nuttall oak that he special ordered from a sustainable nursery for a special price, which happened to be his small nursery. Heck, for an extra $500 he could get to planting it that day and be done quickly.

Most people in the area were rich, so he knew they often happily paid extra to solve problems fast.

The arborist's business grew for several years backed by the lies and alibis perpetuated by the toxic mix. Plus, he was good at choosing reliable, cheap, desperate, illegal laborers to get the tough work of hedging hedges, weeding weeds, and other elements of landscaping that he would not do because he was an arborist, a tree surgeon.

He'd been to college, first in his family, and got a degree in biology and botany. It was the trees he'd loved working with, but desperate to pay child support due to an affair, with a botanist, he'd made his toxic mix and set about poisoning the trees he claimed to love. The affair'd begun under an old oak tree.

Rando if you don't know (X)

HELLO
Apple.
Wolf.
Ball.
Uh oh!

THE MIGHTY OAK

"Why would you do that," the neighbor demanded.

"The tree had rot," the man said.

"No, the tree you just chopped down on to my garage was alive and well last time I checked," the neighbor said. "Look! The leaves are still green. We could have called an arborist."

"The core was rotten," the man said.

"You're joking, right? Look at those rings," the neighbor said pointing to the stump. "Does that look rotten to you?"

"It was a fungus. Had to be chopped."

"You needlessly destroyed a piece of nature so you can get a better view. You destroyed my garage."

"Got homeowner's?"

"That's not the point. You trespassed on my land. You defied a court order saying leave the tree alone."

"Semantics, we knew that tree had to come down."

"It was a mighty oak like the tree expert said."

"White fungus was killing it from the inside plus there were vermin."

"Squirrels! Come on. Every tree has squirrels and lives."

"This one won't anymore."

"That's it. I am suing you for destruction of property,

and I am telling the city and they'd better give you a big fine. That's the only way you'll listen."

"That's not very neighborly."

"What's neighborly at this point?"

"Helping to make firewood."

"That's some nerve you've got," the neighbor said and stormed off.

The man reached for his chainsaw and cranked it.

Rando if you don't know (XI)

ENERGY

I need that energy yo
I need that get up and go
I need that great growing flow
. . . you know

(And then it hits)

TRANSATLANTIC FOOTBRIDGE

The beach grew gray as the howling wind lashing the faces of weekend pleasure seekers interrupted their fun. The pleasure seekers packed up their possessions and sought shelter. A lone man ventured forth toward the beach excusing himself to beg a moment of the pleasure seekers' time while they dashed to their refuges.

"Excuse me, do you know where the Transatlantic footbridge is?"

Replies to the lone man's query included:

- "What? Are you crazy? There's a storm coming."
- "I don't know somewhere over that way."
- "I've never heard of such a thing."

A thud of thunder and crackle of lightning drew perilously closer. The timing between the two grew shorter as the storm drew to shore.

The lone unshaven man's eyes looked worn from a lack of sleep. But he wore a crisply-pressed pair of khakis and a light blue shirt, which he left unbuttoned at the top. With a pack slung over his back, he appeared ready for an expedition.

The lone man asked one straggler the direction to the Transatlantic footbridge.

"No, I'm afraid I don't," the straggler said pausing to reflect. "Are you sure that exists?"

"Oh yes," the lone man said. "Why I have on good word from a Frenchman that it's somewhere in the area. I can't remember where the Frenchie said exactly as I have lost my bearings."

"It sounds interesting enough," said the straggler. "Say I don't suppose you want to join me the in pub over there for a drink and tell me out it. This storm coming in looks like it might last a while and I have to wait it out to collect some crab traps offshore."

"I could. If you know the waters like it sounds you do, then maybe you can help me."

"Alright why not? Let's go. My name is Mark Forester. What's yours?"

"Joe Marlin, pleased to meet you."

The two shook hands assessing each other.

"Likewise, the pub's just over here."

They walked and exchanged further pleasantries before entering the pub called Periwinkles. The bar was made of thousands of periwinkles glued and shellacked together. The top of the bar was covered in glass to protect the casing of sand strewn with shells and starfish throughout to give off the feeling of drinking at the beach.

The atmosphere didn't live up to the expectations. Periwinkles was dimly lit to shade the few glum faces occupying space. The air was smoky from poor ventilation and amply-smoked cigarettes. The smoke created a stale smell topped over salty air and a strong scent of overused deep fryers.

"Hey Shirley, crappy weather, huh?" Forester said to the barmaid upon taking a seat with Marlin.

"Forester, you're getting out of the rain," Shirley said as the sky pumped ample amounts of water onto the earth. "You gonna spend some time with me then?"

"Looks like it," Forester said looking out pub's window.

It poured heavily and one barely saw five feet outside the pub's window.

"I see you brought a friend," Shirley said.

"Yeah, this is Joe Marlin, I convinced him to wait out the storm with me."

Marlin looked around the bar, but quickly turned to gaze upon Shirley and acknowledge her with a friendly smile and nod. He pulled out a pack of cigarettes and threw them on the bar after pulling one out to light up.

"Pleasure to meet you," Shirley said. "What are you fellas having?"

"How about two pints, please? Does that sound good to you Marlin?"

"Shoot yeah," Marlin said after exhaling a large puff.

"Just a sec," Shirley said going over to the tap and pouring out two tall glasses of frothy beer. She dropped off the drinks and left.

That awkward moment of silence crept in after the two took big swigs from their glasses and put them down.

Forester interjected, "What were you on about asking where the Transatlantic footbridge was?"

"Only perhaps the greatest feat of construction ever completed. The Transatlantic footbridge is a hidden path that connects the continents of North America and Europe, and it's all under water."

"Don't you mean that land bridge that the ancestors of the Indians took from Russia into Alaska during the Ice Age?"

"Nope, this is an entirely different structure. It still exists. At least that's what a Frenchman told me and I believe him. That's why I'm looking for it now because I intend to cross it."

"Why not take a plane or a boat?"

"I don't fly and there's no adventure in a boat these days. No sir, I want to get to Europe and the bridge is the only way I'm going."

"I can't fathom such a thing. I mean if it existed, wouldn't boats run into it all the time and wreck it. There'd be boats with holes in their hulls if there was a bridge in the middle of the ocean."

"It's an underwater bridge."

"You mean a tunnel."

"Not quite. It's underwater and encapsulated like a tunnel, but you can still fall off. It's a giant swing bridge in parts and floats with the whims of the current tethered only at two points. Somewhere around here and at the other end on the shores of France."

"Surely if it's underwater you would get the bends from too much pressure."

"No amazingly, it's pressurized and that's the least of your worries."

"Sounds far-fetched to me."

"I had my doubts two days ago, but I know it's there and I aim to cross it. The bridge is perilous, but the journey extraordinary."

Marlin began explaining how he learned about the bridge. Two days before Marlin was sweeping the beach with his metal detector before dusk looking for loose change and any other valuables the pleasure seekers may have left. Marlin had plenty of money and had retired at an early age.

He trolled the beaches to fill the void in his life ever since his wife Ursula drowned offshore during a freak storm some years ago.

He was about to give up his efforts satisfied with about five dollars in change and a silver-plated bracelet when he turned to glance at the sea. A fully-dressed man with long curly hair bunched up from the ocean water emerged from the sea soaked to his thin bones in a blue sweater and combat pants. The seafarer wore no shoes and carried a large leather satchel. Marlin approached the man thinking perhaps he had survived a boating accident.

Marlin asked the man if he was alright and if he needed any help. The man breathed heavily and upon leaving the water collapsed onto the beach exhausted. However, he had a great look of glee and enjoyment on his face. He began to laugh and raise his fists in exaltation while speaking a foreign tongue. Marlin stood over the man not knowing what to make of him.

A few moments passed until the man caught his breath. He looked up and saw Marlin with a curious look.

"Monsieur," the man said, "tell me, where I am."

Marlin said the east coast of the United States.

Marlin asked if he had been in a shipwreck.

"No," the man replied in broken English with a heavy French accent, saying that he had completed an extraordinary journey that was too difficult to explain. Apparently, he was the first man in modern times to do it.

"What do you mean?" Marlin asked.

The man got up and brushed some of the sand from his clothes. The man apologized and asked for a cigarette.

Marlin gave the man a cigarette and lit one too.

"Monsieur," the man said, "I am Antoine Delamer."

Marlin introduced himself and asked the man to explain. One doesn't usually pop out of the sea claiming to have finished an extraordinary journey.

Delamer took a huge drag on the cigarette and assessed his situation. "Monsieur," he said humbly, "could you give me some food and clothes and I promise you will not be disappointed."

Or that was the best that Marlin could translate in his mind what Delamer was saying in such an outrageous French accent.

"Why not?" Marlin said.

In Marlin's car, they drove to the house Marlin rented for the past two months, which was located approximately at the exact parallel place on land where Ursula had perished at sea some time ago.

Delamer was amicable on the drive, asking Marlin many questions about news and events of the world. Marlin answered Delamer's questions as best he could and wondered how Delamer didn't know about so many stories that captured the headlines of the world for more than a year. It took some time as Delamer struggled to speak English fluidly and often paused to look for a word. Sometimes Delamer asked Marlin to repeat himself more slowly.

In the house, Marlin showed an appreciative Delamer to the shower and quickly whipped up a batch of spaghetti.

After some time Delamer entered the kitchen wearing some old clothes Marlin gave him. The clothes hung loose on Delamer because he was so thin. The sleeves rose above his wrists. Delamer used an impromptu piece of string to hold up his sagging pants. He looked like the remnants of a deflated ball.

Marlin served the spaghetti. They ate in silence as Delamer wolfed down two plates of pasta. Delamer apologized for his poor manners saying he hadn't eaten a real meal in ages. Finally satisfied, Delamer pushed the plate away, and asked Marlin for another cigarette saying he had forgotten the pleasures of land.

"Wait so you let a total stranger into your house?" Forester said after ordering another round from Shirley. "You must be a good man. This guy sounds like a total bum."

"Like I said I had my doubts, but then he pulled out this relic."

"Monsieur, I thank you so much for your hospitality and I will prove to you that I have crossed the Transatlantic footbridge," Delamer said.

Marlin offered to light his cigarette, but Delamer laughed saying, "*Ce n'est pas necessaire.*" Delamer pulled from his drenched satchel a glob of seaweed. Delamer put the glob on the table and proceeded to peel away the layers. Inside was small smooth rock with strangely detailed markings all over.

Delamer asked Marlin to hold the rock and examine it. Marlin looked closely noticing the rock's markings, which appeared to be strange writings. Delamer explained that the rock was a gift from a friend he met in the sea.

"Watch," Delamer said.

Delamer took the rock and held it in the palm of his right hand. Then he licked his left index finger and swabbed the rock with his finger to remove a glint of black residue. Delamer showed his finger to Marlin and then offered a wink and a smile before rubbing his thumb against his finger. Marlin wasn't sure what the Frenchman was doing.

A spark ignited a fire on the tip of Delamer's finger which

he used to light the cigarette. Marlin looked in amazement, but wondered if it was a cheap magic trick.

Delamer said the rock was a lava rock from the core of the Earth that a friend gave him during his time in the Marinas Trench—the deepest part of the sea nearly twice the length of Mt. Everest from the surface of the Earth where it was always thought no one had ever been before.

"May I?" Marlin asked with piqued curiosity.

Delamer handed the rock to Marlin before taking a drag from his cigarette.

Marlin looked at the rock and then licked his finger, rubbed the rock to attain some residue. Marlin put his finger and thumb together still skeptical and began to rub. After a moment a spark burst forth and then a flame. Marlin was shocked to see the tip of his finger on fire, yet he felt no heat.

"It is amazing, *non*?" Delamer said with a big grin.

Marlin took his eyes off the flame and nodded to Delamer. Marlin turned his attention back to the flame and watched it dance some more before going out. He tried the rock again and got the same effect. Delamer said that the rock had saved him from the cold depths of the sea many times and worked reasonably well as a way to cook fish and boil seaweed. Delamer said the rock had been bigger, but he had used it a lot. However, Delamer noted that the markings always remained.

"What do they mean?" Marlin asked.

Delamer said some sea language that he could never master.

Intrigued, Marlin asked who gave Delamer the rock.

Delamer said a fellow human. Some shipwreck survivor who had sunk all the way down to the Trench.

"What?" Marlin asked.

Delamer explained that certain people at the right moment of the tides drowned. However, upon falling into the trench other people who had suffered the same fate revived the drowned in a way that allowed them to live, but they could never return to land. Delamer said that it was a practice that had been going on for ages and, like on earth, no one had a definite explanation as to how they had come into being. "Unfortunately," Delamer said, "to live under the sea the people must breath with water. If these people resurfaced, they would die as fish out of water."

Marlin thought of Ursula. What if…? Marlin wanted to know everything about Delamer's adventure and inundated him with questions.

"How did Delamer as a human survive under the sea?"

"With these," Delamer said, pulling out two small conch shells and fastened them snugly in his ears. Delamer said the shells dealt with the initial pressure upon entering the bridge and added that for most parts the bridge was effectively covered so that one didn't need a breathing apparatus though he recommended a snorkel for emergencies. For food Delamer simply said that the sea was full of fish and seaweed, though he added there is no spice besides salt. Delamer said the most important thing to take was a desalinization kit, which was basically two small pots and fine strainer he used to get fresh water by boiling. Delamer said it was another world altogether, but that the human body was surprisingly adaptable to the environment. "Besides," Delamer said, "the farther you get down the more creatures and people you will meet with provisions."

They stayed up until dawn as Delamer explained the various facets of his journey, including the ways he survived and the many perils he faced on the bridge. Marlin was totally enthralled and listened to every detail. Only after Delamer said he needed sleep did Marlin cease asking questions. After showing Delamer to his bed, Marlin remained awake wracked with questions wondering about the possibility of reuniting with his lost love.

Marlin slept late into the afternoon. He awoke groggy, unsure if he had dreamed up the whole affair. After brushing his teeth, he entered the living room and called out to Delamer. There was no answer. Marlin looked everywhere in the house. Perhaps he has gone for a walk, Marlin thought while going to the kitchen for a cup of coffee. That was when he noticed the note on the table held in place by two small conch shells with a lava rock next to it. The note was addressed to Marlin, but it was written in French. Apparently Delamer couldn't write in English. Marlin tried to read the letter but made no sense of it.

Without thinking, Marlin grabbed the letter and quickly left in his car for the local library where Marlin found an old French to English dictionary and roughly translated the letter:

Cher Monsieur Marlin,

Thank you so much for your kind hospitality. Upon reading the paper and assessing the state of the land, I have decided to return to the sea. There I think I can make a real difference. I am sorry to have mentioned my adventures to you. I know you are curious to know if your wife is below the sea, but I beg you not to follow for I can guarantee you nothing. If you must go, then take coins if you can, everybody likes shiny things down there since a ray of the sun is so rare. The way down is a lot easier than the ascension.

The ocean is like a liquid desert. Don't forget the desalinization kit. Without it you will die. Please I trust you will tell the details of my story to as few people as possible. The bridge is perilous, but the journey *extraordinaire*.

Sincèrement,

Antoine Delamer

On the letter's back, a quickly drawn map pointed to the entrance to the footbridge and an even rougher roadmap with a few seamarks designated.

"Wow that's quite a story Joe," Forester said looking at the letter and then carefully studying the map on the back. "I don't know it's still crazy and farfetched if you ask me. Hey maybe the storm's about to pass."

"I know it sounds crazy, but I have nothing to stay for. When Ursula drowned, so did I. This is the one chance that makes any sense to me. I want to take her to Paris like I always promised. I know that sounds irrational, but I don't care. The problem is the map is only so useful, I can't remember exactly where we were when Delamer came ashore. I think I am looking for an opening on the sea floor that will lead me down to the bridge."

"There's this hole just offshore that the old mariners say is bottomless. But it's a bunch of shenanigans. Some underwater cave. No one knows for sure it's supposed to have a curse and there's a dangerous tidal pool near it so no one ventures there long."

"Are you serious? That has to be it. I beg you please show me where it is."

"I don't know. You seem sound of mind, but what you're talking about is madness and I would hate to see you drown."

"Please, I would never hold you responsible if anything happened to me. I'll sign a waiver. You must take me there."

The storm subsided though the waves remained choppy. Forester relented to Marlin's request after tears of desperation welled up in Marlin's eyes.

Marlin paid the tab and thanked Shirley for her service with a big tip. They hopped in Forester's boat and headed out to sea.

After a knot out or so, Forester pointed to the tidal pool and place where he thought the hole lay below.

Marlin grew excited.

Forester grew nervous thinking he was making a huge mistake, delivering a man to his death.

The flow of the water changed and swirled violently. Forester weighed anchor just outside the edge of the spinning tidal pool. Marlin pulled out a miniature SCUBA kit and explained that he thought he might need it to get down to the opening. Then he handed Forester the keys to his car and said to take it as a payment and anything he wanted in the house. Forester felt terrible and threatened to turn the boat around, but the heartache beset in Marlin's eyes told him that he couldn't ruin a broken man's hopes. After all, Forester thought, I have some of those too.

Concerned that Forester might be changing his mind, Marlin readied his gear. Then Marlin thanked Forester for all of his help and in an instant flopped over the side. Marlin was savagely spun into the tidal pool.

Forester panicked and threw a lifesaver to Marlin.

But Marlin didn't try to catch it and instead spun deeper into the pool.

Just before vanishing below the surface it appeared Marlin gave Forester a thumbs up or perhaps it was the last struggle of a dying life.

Rando if you do know (I)

SUPER NUMBER 1

Only buy, participate in, listen to, watch, do whatever is ranked number 1 or most popular in the field of your choice. See how life changes.

WILLIAMSTOWN BEACH?

On the elevator up to work, David spoke with the new intern Rachel whom he found attractive. She looked hip with a crisply coiffed hairdo, flushed cheeks, and green eyes. She had three arms, and wore a special blue fitting shirt. David hadn't noticed the third arm before, but whatever.

Rachel said she was from Williamstown, Massachusetts, where David's friend Linda hailed. They got off the elevator with Rachel talking about Williamstown's scene. She stopped, and said she was waiting for another Vice President.

Lingering and listening somewhat, David recalled how he had been to Williamstown a few years back with several friends to visit Linda. They'd gone to the beach in an SUV where they had a party, until the police showed up asking them to leave. But there was no beach in Western Mass. Not the salt kind at least. Everyone stayed at Linda's mom's house, which was a McMansion with plenty of rooms. David's dad, Ron, appeared unexpectedly asking David to fix his computer.

David's friends went to the County Fair, but he decided to drive back to the beach, where cars were parked on a windy dirt road walled by thick trees on both sides on the way to the beach.

David found a parking spot between two large decked out suvs.

A channel cut the beach with a swift current leading into an interior moving through a lush mangrove. David swam in the channel letting the current take him away. It felt nice initially floating along, switching as new channels of water appeared, and he chose left or right going deeper into the stream through the mangrove. It wasn't Williamstown, for sure. Where was he?

The current grew stronger, but David liked it. A whirling mix of water came fast, maybe an eddy. He swam hard right to avoid getting sucked in, but a stronger current took him left and spun him around.

David blacked out and woke up in the rain on a set of broken wooden steps going nowhere.

Linda found David. She had her family with her. She asked him what happened. He said remembered nothing since the whirling water. They decided David must have suffered a concussion.

Linda's family got in some car, while Linda and David got in an old, boxy yellow Toyota. It was Linda's cousin's, and the tire walls were caked in thick red mud, uncommon to those parts. Like her cousin had gone four-wheeling, but how in a tiny Toyota?

The road back from the beach was muddy, but the mud was black. The seats were cramped. David felt confused. They drove back to Linda's mom's place.

That night he ensured he took off his nicotine patch before sleeping.

David turned back to reality.

Three-arm Rachel was gone.

WISDOM IN TEA?

"Have a cup of tea. It will soothe your soul."

Or that's what she said pouring the steaming water from the kettle into my cup. My choices were chamomile, mint, lemon, or green. I went for green and let the bag steep for the recommended time of four minutes.

We settled in, anticipating the tea and smiling at one another knowing that something could be resolved. Honey or not? Sweeten it up or go full throttle into the bleak void of the green.

Go for it.

Crush the watery steam with a blow or two.

Cooler now. Look up, and then test it.

No, not too hot.

Sip, embrace, swallow, cleanse.

Repeat, if only briefly, and feel renewed and restored.

Now what?

Leave the cup and get down to it.

What was it?

MR. EXACTLY

Some parallel world where when you feel threatened, the spirit of a friend arrives and wards the threat(s) away, such as Marvin, when some similar dude comes to threaten. Indochina and on tour; visited cave. At hotel, kept feeling car was getting stolen.

Earlier got into car with a white waiter who threw a paper ball at me (on the street for no reason). Maybe it was a bill I'd forgotten to pay. Sights kept changing. I had to question reality. Walking, exploring (place?). Also: Callie and Scott briefly talking and lying to each other on phone. Lots of kids.

At the start I am in decrepit office building near some airport with two people, one possibly Mike Wheeler. Long rows and we're walking, talking, and exploring. We find a bunch of digital cameras (I think this took place in a long narrow abandoned house). I take one (camera) but can't close it. I go outside and there's a Thai family looking at me, and I feel guilty perhaps because I can't say hello and thank you in their language (*sawatdi* and *khopkhun*).

A little girl helps me with the camera, and then there is a distraction when an expat in a tricked-out Bentley with dragon designs pulls up.

Then I'm exploring a town with two women in some other country.

Next, I'm in a bar mentioning that I only plan to go to India and Thailand. A patron talks about his home country and the town of Jidda. He pulls out a map and shows me where it is.

Place where I saw the cave was there, as was lodge where I shared a room with this woman and we needed towels. (Vaguely remember seeing map of countries on Earth that connect but do not exist, and maybe from previous experience but remember plotting points all over faux continent with plans to go exploring).

In a hotel bar. I carried on conversations which I do not recall with a mother and her child, but the conversations felt strange, but appropriate. We headed back to our rooms on the same corridor through this long hallway that felt eerily like that decrepit office building. We passed people and a few unfolding scenes. Then we're outside. I check to see if my car is there. It is, but then it's gone. Then it's there. Back and forth with every different angle. Nobody cares. Security forces appear blasé.

These aggressive people come towards us. They look like friends somewhat, but then the spirit of the real friend, Marvin, comes along and wards them off. That's when I woke up in America.

Something went wrong.

WATER BUFFALO IN AMERICA

It's often overlooked in U.S. history, but the water buffalo went the way of the buffalo even faster than their Native American brethren. Water buffalo were imported from Asia in the late nineteenth century, coming over with the many Asian laborers who cherished them as symbols of good luck, or so legend might have it.

Have you seen their faces? They're so cute and docile. Surely, they could do no harm?

The water buffalo soon inhabited vast tracts of land in the Midwest, but locals paid them little attention because the water buffalo blended in with what was left of the decimated native buffalo population. However, the water buffalo had one major need the natives did not. Water and lots of it!

This need is eventually what led to the great American dust bowl in the early twentieth century, where so many farmers went under, in a dusty sense. It was largely attributed to drought, but the real strain came from the growing population of water buffalo in need of voluminous quantities to satiate their huge thirst to absorb as much water as possible.

Why else would they be called water buffalo?

A clued-in scientist finally realized the devastation these feral beasts caused. A solution, some might say a final saline solution, was hatched in a Kansas City, Missouri, lab specializing in salt licks.

Teams with special salt licks made of an untested sodium derivative devised to create extreme thirst, originally created by beer companies, but deemed too dangerous for human consumption, were dispatched in planes throughout the midwest with intentions of dropping pellets of these salt licks all over the fields of wherever the water buffalo may roam.

The scheme worked, water buffalo were no longer a concern, and Italian restaurants felt secure knowing they could charge extra for real Italian buffalo mozzarella with the American competition no longer a concern.

Rando if you do know (I.5)

B.O.B.

Big Owl Bert
This is not the story of Bob,
but rather baby Bob.
Hooting softly.
Warm in a nest.
Lots of regurgitated food.
Mother tends the babes.
Later, Bob flies away.

DINOSAUR EYES

Walking on an unnamed island off the New Jersey Coast, the view was foggy and murky.

Bedecked in full uniform, a Coast Guard guy stood next to a suit-and-hat-wearing detective next to me. They planned to set up a new prison on the island's old prison ground.

An outspoken nurse once claimed to have died from cancer from working there. Whispers flourished about chemicals. But then one always asked how the nurse said she died, if she was alive.

Some shady fishermen appeared near the shoreline. The detective asked their business receiving vague utterances. The fishermen turned, and there was no way to follow them. The Coast Guard guy noted their wake.

We walked along a narrow path where you'd have to time it with the waves to go forward.

High tide kept rising.

The detective wandered ahead. The Coast Guard guy stopped me, and said, "Dinosaur eyes, gosh look at those dinosaur eyes."

I started to look down. The detective ran back in a rush waving us away.

I fainted.

BLOODY CASTLE

An ancient castle faltered, run over by vines and weeds with stonework failing to hold back the ravages of time set away from an old trail immersed in woods surrounded by nature.

Some time ago, many great conquerors focused on conquering the castle since it served as a hub for trade when tongues were used differently.

Forgotten, save for the few who scavenged for lime rock in the area. The castle, they said, was cursed.

They say it started in that ancient time when a young prince took a hallucinogen.

It ended with the decapitation of a king thought to be a mocking deer.

Apparently, all was a conjured spell, caste out by a craggy, old witch hoping to regain the youth of a lost lover once thwarted by the headless king.

Such was the time of an epic battle forged in iron and steel with great warriors casting aside good warriors, while their steads, maidens, minstrels, and muses, among others, wished for better, more peaceful times.

But the blood always flowed in the river by the castle.

So much blood that soon after the king lost his head and the prince executed for murder did the whole castle's population run afoul with bad water, bloody water, or was it the curse of the predictor for what killed them all?

Gareth knew none of these tales of woe when he happened upon the castle by accident on a hot, sunny day going for a swim with his friends Adrian and Steve.

Needless to say, it got bloody real fast.

Rando if you don't know (XII)

GREAT SOUNDS

When the water retreats and the rocks roll down before the waves crash in again.

TRADING DAYS

Stan (not his real name), the stock picker, looked for winners by picking losers. But the investors never knew with the act:

- pressed suit;
- red power tie;
- monogrammed tie (S.V.D.);
- flashy smile;
- fresh tan to make his eyes sparkle;
- confident posture;
- honed words about being a man;
- deep diving, circuitous answers to any tough, questioning questions; and
- talk of Miami, sexy women and the Fontainebleau or better.

"You'll know soon," he promised. "Just go with me."

"Look at this," he'd say next showing a good enough financial statement to not be true, but whet the appetites of the dumbs, as he called them, for titillating possibilities. "This could be you."

Seven figures showing, they'd say, "please."

Always, or enough for Stan to lead a taste of the lifestyle they all coveted.

Dumbs with $5-20k looking to play the market thought they could somehow convert chump change into upper class with the trust of Stan, and yes, he said, "I'm your man."

The dumbs heard someone else did that well.

Everyone dares to dream, and Stan figured out how to sell the dumbs their dreams to them for himself.

Everything went great with a few shell companies, a lawyer friend and a change of address and business move. An LLC only cost $90 in Delaware.

Soon enough for Stan, he started socking away for his dream of a bar in the Bahamas, despite an upset phone call here and there from, say, an angry wife. But it was her husband's fault, never Stan's.

All until she walked in looking to invest $500k cash like she knew what she was doing . . .

Rando if you don't know (XII.5)

AMPHIBIANS

Are you croaking?
Who is Crow King?
What? No dying.
Why are you so funny? Like a frog?
How do you mean?
When were you speaking about?
Where?
There . . .
Exactly.
Now, I'm confused.

THE SEVENTH SEA

You see we're headed for the seventh sea.
For the other six we've been to plus the Sea of Galilee.
But the seventh sea is a mystery,
upon which we must solve.
No sand nor landlubber they say ever touches
its chest that makes it a mess,
and if is only a sea upon a sea or a sea within a sea
'tis what we must get to thee!
Now fir we are on a quest, and we never rest
until we cross the chest and crest
into the seventh sea that's best
for treasure awaits the divine
and death the rest.
Come with me if ye can be diviner than the Divinity.
I read this a mess
eyeing an empty whiskey glass.
Alas down it goes,
and in my throes
I did follow the Captain on his quest
and quicker than I expected seen
in a golden crystal dream
a seventh sea upon the tide.
I'd ride down to hell for nary a mind.

PACIFIC STREET

Booming bass beat from a tricked-out orange 1993 Honda Civic owned by Terrell "Tigger" Taylor, sometimes called Triple Threat.

Tigger stood nearby shifting confidently back and forth in an energetic bounce amongst his crew: Bunny, Crick, and Krush.

"This is where it kicks," Tigger said about the jam on the stereo. "Oh yeah, you feel dat?"

"That's sweet," Krush said.

They'd blazed through a blunt and grew mellow, content to survey the block they considered their turf. No one had bothered to question their reign supreme with Terrell on top since 2011 when the little man got got, as they'd said. No one searched too hard for the little man trying to claim a piece of a block few cared about anyway.

Gina sashayed along in high heels and a tight pink mini skirt. Her hooped gold earrings jangled when she shot a smile at Tigger and the boys before keeping on.

"Damn, I gots to get me some a dat," Tigger said.

"We all do," Bunny said.

Krush and Crick giggled.

"Come on, Bunny, it ain't gonna be like that. She too fine for runnin' trains not like that bitch Tamara," Tigger said.

"Then you best get that while you can son, cause if you won't, I will," Krush said.

"Oh, it's on, killa," Tigger said with a smirk and hustled over to Gina, who looked over but kept walking.

Tigger kept pace and gave her the vertical assessment.

"You looking fine girl," Tigger said. "Why don't you let me get up wit you?"

"You sure you got the mark," Gina said stopping and returning the up and down favor. "I know you think you do."

"I do, don't be playin'."

"Maybe we can play later, but I got to get to court right now," Gina said.

"You gonna let me call you?"

"Go on then call me tomorrow."

"You know I will," Tigger said, smiling and returning to his boys.

Terrell looked assured as he strode over to get a fist bump from Crick.

"I'm gonna be up in that soon," Terrell said. "I can't wait son, she's gotta have a ..."

Water splashed all over Tigger from a water balloon. Another hit Crick. Bunny and Krush took shelter under a tree. Another balloon soaked Tigger.

Furious, he looked up and spotted the balloon's launch site. He figured it was one of the smaller kids from the block, but they should know better. He'd teach them.

"This ain't gonna stand," Tigger said and took off to one of the fire escapes quickly scaling up and up to the top of the five-story building as he'd often done before he ruled his street. He breathed heavy when he neared the top. He paused to catch his breath, but felt ready to rumble.

Another water balloon was lobbed.

"That's it," Tigger said, "nobody be messing about like that on this block."

Tigger crested onto the roof and was met square by a bullet between the eyes. He fell back and plummeted to the street. His body thudded on the sidewalk.

"Oh shit Tig!" Krush screamed.

They checked. He was dead.

Police arrived ten minutes later.

Detective Strickland showed up an hour later in a foul mood nursing a hangover and feeling unsavory effects of a stale Danish and bad coffee work his innards. He wanted a little dog hair, and reached into his black leather jacket for his flask. It wasn't there. Did he lose it last night? He couldn't remember, like most nights. He didn't want to wait on his partner, Artie, who was running late from a dental appointment. Get to it, he thought.

Strickland inquired with the beat cops on what they knew, then looked up at the fire escape then back to where Tigger had landed. Blood stains remained, but the coroner had removed the body.

Several onlookers speculated what happened while cops took statements. Nobody saw anyone come down and no one had bothered to go up to the roof.

Strickland decided he would, and got the building's super to take him up via the stairs.

Brooklyn spread out in all directions. Yellowing trees dotted in amongst the buildings on the crisp autumn day. The super lingered by while Strickland paced around looking for any clues, maybe a shell casing or a footprint. Nothing, although Strickland decided a forensics crew should take a finer comb to the roof. Several buildings connected making a thorough-fare for the killer to take off either way. Strickland noticed a wet graffiti tag. His finger was black with fresh spray paint after he touched it. Stepping back, he saw in a scrawling script, "D-Bop!"

Strickland contemplated the meaning, and then called for backup before traipsing over the roofs. He stopped when he reached a garden. It was out of place, but the gentrifiers had been putting gardens on top of buildings for ecological benefits here and there, so it made sense.

Maybe a garden hose was the source for the water balloons, Strickland speculated and then noticed more D-Bop! tags.

Back on the street, Strickland instructed the beat cops to ask about D-Bop! to see if anyone knew who sprayed those tags or what it meant.

Artie showed up in a hoodie with his badge hang-ing round his neck on a chain. Strickland noted Artie's Chuck Taylors and thought he was getting too used to being casual in plain clothes. How could he run in those things?

Strickland recalled when Artie was a beat a few years back, but his daddy had gotten him up the chain faster than most. Still he was a good cop and partner, except for being a teetotaler. Strickland never quite trusted a man who couldn't handle a drink, even worse were the ones who wouldn't drink. Artie said it had something to do with his teenage days that he was sober now, but never expanded on it, not that Strickland asked.

"Terrell Taylor looks to be a piece a shit that anybody could have wanted dead," Artie said. "He's got a long rap, in and out of juvenile detention and onto a few stints upstate for drugs and theft, and just back from a few months on Rikers for assault. Now dead at twenty-four."

"Sounds like a fine fella," Strickland said.

"And the killer?" Artie asked.

"Maybe D-Bop! whatever that means," Strickland said. "There was a fresh tag up there, but I don't know if anyone would be so stupid as to tag right where they murdered."

"Plenty of dumb criminals."

"I got the boys to try and figure out who sprays D-Bop! The tags are everywhere topside so if it ain't the killer then maybe they saw something. Looks like the water balloons got filled from a spigot from a garden on top of a building a few doors down that way," Strickland said pointing before reaching for an e-cigarette.

After inhaling and blowing out the fake smoke, Strickland continued, "We should canvas the area, see what's up with this scene lately, where these guys go and who knows what."

"The homeboys are playing dumb. They're upset about Terrell, or Tigger as they call him, but they say they don't know nothing."

"Nothing new there," Strickland said taking another deep inhale.

ECUADOREAN ROOT CANAL

The next time I torture someone, I'm definitely using dental equipment. The amount of pain I've been through is downright unbearable. I bet if I get some drills and pins going up one's molars, I could get anyone to start confessing their deepest secrets quick. Maybe I'd even offer to patch them up with some filler afterwards. Of course, I'd have to learn how to do that one first.

My profession doesn't typically go in for dental hygiene. But here I am working in Quito, Ecuador, or not working at all thanks to my damn back, upper, right molar being aflame. I've been in the process of finalizing a root canal down here for the past week. And it's been meditative cause it's the least of my worries.

I should have known this whole trip was a bad idea when they lost my luggage for a day and the cab driver ripped me off for ten bucks. It's not the money, it's the damn principle.

Used to be no one ever got over on me, anywhere, anytime, anyplace. You tried to mess with me, you'd be reprimanded sooner or later. But I'm older now and clearly getting slower and softer. Like my hometown, baby. NYC. It's for pussies now. I reckon Philly or Baltimore is where the tough guys are today, but I'd never tell any of those squishy fucks that.

Quito has done a number on me. But it's been coming for a while. Some coach would tell me my head isn't in the game anymore. And it's not, I'll admit. I've got different priorities. I got bills for my kid's college to think about and I've got my dreams going strong for when I get out. And I want out sooner rather than never. Those are the only two options when it comes to a guy like me.

That or getting butt fucked in prison. No, thank you.

No, I got my eye on setting up a bait shop in the Finger Lakes. Maybe even buying a little piece of land to start practicing what they call vermiculture. It's basically a worm farm.

Of course, I need to figure out more things about the nutrients and right acid levels of dirt. Hell, I don't know what kind of bait is best for the Finger Lakes. I've only been fishing a few times, and never upstate, usually Jamaica Bay. And that's a whole different beast. Plus, it's not like you want to eat any of that shit anyway. With what you catch in there, God knows what it is and where it's been.

My friend John caught some fish in the Bay once, and found a finger in the fish's belly with a wedding ring on it. John kept the ring to pawn and threw away the fish.

Hell, that finger could have been one of my earlier pieces of work. I was sloppier back then.

But I'm supposed to be professional level. Smooth in and out. No problems. I've been on so many of these over-seas jobs over the past years, and never a hitch until the last one. And then here I am in Quito all fucked up every which way, and I got to sit in this damn dentist's chair and take one more session of poking, drilling, prodding, tooth fucking, and everything.

At least it's the last session, and overall Dr. M's been super-efficient and nice. I hope I don't have to kill her. Nah, I don't want to and shouldn't be necessary.

I'm a sick, twisted fuck. I don't kill for fun. I take no joy in it. It's work. And I clock in and clock out. Or at least I used to. Man, why can't I get Rio out of my head. I should never take a job in South America ever again. But here I am in freaking Ecuador.

Like I was saying, the trip was a screw up to begin with. Don told me it was an easy gig, no killing only some dealings with some friendly types and scoping out a few places for future work potential maybe. It was going to be a little equatorial vacation, Don said. I could chill out, check out a nice city, and maybe get some nice things for Clara.

That's how it was supposed to be. The signal should have been the burgeoning pain in my tooth on the plane. I chalked it up to altitude, and took a Vicodin and whiskey to sooth the ache. I'd been drinking more than usual and popping pills 'cause they helped delude my thoughts.

But I see the booze and pills are making me soft and weak. To hell with them, I got to stay sharp.

I got through customs easy. I even used my real passport 'cause everything was to be above board. No bullshit. Michael Brevard. *Si. Que es* something the reason for your visit. *Turismo.* Okay that's about as far as I got before we had to switch to English. I probably should have tried harder with the Spanish when I was married to my ex, Gloria.

She's Puerto Rican and boy did she have a sweet ass and some serious heat back in the day. Now I think she's strung out on Oxy. She used to try to teach me stuff so I could impress her Papi, or at least attempt to do so. But I never had an ear for languages. I can read a menu and all in a few languages. But I don't think Papi ever gave me a chance. I don't think he wanted his daughter marrying some *pindao gringo*, as I heard him call every fucking visit.

Maybe I should have asked Gloria for some tips last time I saw her, but she was too strung out. Which makes me worry about my, our, daughter Clara, but she'll pull through.

Clara's almost out of that damn house that I bought and paid for, but haven't lived in more than ten years. I still remember marking Clara's height on the kitchen walls. She's a looker boy, just like her Mama. But way smarter, and she's on the books big time. Off to Tufts this fall. That is if I can pay the damn tuition and board. Man, it's pricey, and that's why I'm down here in god damn Quito cause I got to make sure my baby's taken care of. It's the least I can do since I wasn't there for her much since Gloria and I split. But that's going to change. Maybe she can come and hang out and work in the bait shop in the summers. Probably not, but if I get a little place and get a garden going and some nice furniture, she'll come. I know it.

Ouch! *Mucho dolor*, or much pain I tell Dr. M. She's tooth fucking me again, and it damn well hurts cause the anesthetic hasn't kicked in yet. This happens every time, but she's doing her thing working on my tooth and blabbing on the phone at the same time. How she does it without a dental hygienist I don't know. But I guess it keeps the overhead lower and makes it cheaper, which is good for me.

A guy like me doesn't have a dental plan.

I have no package of benefits. $295 for the whole thing, four sessions, included and all. If I weren't in a bind down here in so many other ways, I'd get even more work done. Dr. M tells me I've got three more cavities that she could fill. Or she tells me through Google translate anyway. But I got no time for more fillings. I write back and hit the translate button saying if it can wait, I'll put it off, just the emergency stuff *por favor*. There's plenty of drilling to do anyway. I've got to lie there and take it again. Hell, that's what I've been doing on this whole freaking trip.

Rando if you do know (II)

LESS THANK TWO YARDS DEEP

"I got my hands on my hips, covered in mud, looking like an eighteen-year-old 'cause I don't know what the fuck I'm doing." Yet another ill-planned grave digging by Robert.

BOXED IN

Can't see a thing. It's so dark. I feel trapped in something. It smells like burnt gasoline. Man, why am I so thirsty? How long have I been out? There's a drip somewhere near. Not that way. Feels like a metal wall. Not that way either. There's the drip. It's cool. I hope it's water. Damn that's not water. It tastes horrible. Rancid! Spit it out! I'm thirsty, I can't see and I'm stuck! None of this is good. BANG! BANG! Something or someone is hitting whatever I'm in. The noise makes my ears ring, and whatever I am in is shifting. Am I in a box or a shipping container maybe? I hear voices, but can't tell the language. Sounds Slavic. Am I in New York still? What's hello in Russian? Or hell Serbian? No, I bet it's those Slovaks from a month ago. What bullshit did I tell them? How am I going to get out of this one? *Ahoj!*

SAVE THE FISH, EAT MORE LOBSTER

Reliable evidence suggests that the main reason the Vikings discovered Greenland and stopped off in North America was a quest for cod. All over the globe the populations of traditionally edible fish have dramatically declined. Current catches bring in undersized fish and smaller yields. I'm not only talking about Charlie the Tuna and saving the dolphins. The threat is very real that soon you may no longer be able to enjoy a freshly caught cut of Mahi Mahi or grouper. Already fishermen (people) go out to sea for longer periods of time and farther away from their home shores to ensure a decent catch. Previously untapped fishing waters, such as the South Atlantic, are being overfished to compensate for the ever-growing demand for a lean healthy choice of protein. Fish is a meat more readily available to both the rich and the poor more than any other. So, if popular fish such as cod are going extinct then what are the weary fishermen to do?

Look deeper. Plethora of fish exist deeper in the seas that before may not have even been considered edible. Quite frankly the deeper down you go in the sea, the weirder looking fish get.

We are very superficial, fickle consumers when it comes to our seafood. Have you seen an anglerfish? Trust me, it isn't pretty. You wouldn't want its gnarling teeth, dangling spine lights, spikes, and ghostly eyes staring back at you on your plate! Perhaps a better example is the Chilean Sea Bass. Sounds lovely doesn't it? Do you think it would whet your appetite, as much, if you knew its real name was the Patagonian Toothfish? Patagonian Toothfish doesn't quite have the same ring to it? Somewhere along the way, a chef or a public relations firm for a seafood company came up with the Chilean Sea Bass. It just rolls of the tongue with a certain pleasantness and feeling of sophistication. One can't say the same for Patagonian Toothfish. So, is there some dastardly conspiracy out there to replace those beautiful fish we know and love to eat, like the red snapper, hmm, with the ghastly hideous fish from the bottoms of the sea, like the Hatchetfish, ooh? Perhaps? That's for you to decide.

A more local example of overfishing for me is the Chesapeake Bay. Due to pollution and overfishing the Chesapeake Bay's fish population has declined significantly for years. The same goes for its once-ample stock of blue crabs. Maryland and Virginia are famous for their crab cakes and other seafood delights taken from the Chesapeake. However, in recent years crab and fish populations have declined so much that seafood companies from Maryland and Virginia have on occasion been known to import seafood from places such as Thailand and slap on a canned in the USA label for authenticity. Now something is inherently wrong with this wee deception to the public, don't you think?

Maine is another seafarer's haven known for its cold waters and fresh lobster. In the 1990s, like other seafood populations, the number of lobsters declined significantly. Where had all the lobsters gone? The catches were getting smaller as well as the size of the lobsters. Had the lobsters finally decided to pack up and move to the warmer waters of Florida?

No, they were being overfished to the point of near extinction. Finally, someone realized, hey if we keep catching lobster at this rate, we won't have any more to sell and the very thing that Maine is most famous for won't exist anymore and thus lead to a huge economic downturn for mighty Maine. Strict rules and regulations were put in place, not without incident. Some may disagree, but these regulations are the main reason why the lobster population in Maine has resurged at an enormous rate and the curmudgeonly crustaceans no longer have to worry about their extinction and get to travel to exotic restaurant fish tanks all over the world before meeting their inevitable demise. Pass the garlic butter, please.

Back to the Chesapeake or more specifically the estuaries and waters which lead to the Bay for another disturbing issue. A few years ago, two Asian Snakehead fish were discovered swimming about in a pond in Crofton, Maryland. What's so bad about that you say? Well this particular fish devours so much food including native fish, that it can destroy a pond's ecosystem. It's not just called a Snakehead fish because it's ugly. The Snakehead fish can uncannily crawl over land from one body of water to another when its tummy gets a yearning for something tasty. The two Snakeheads were caught and killed and it was thought that was that. Alas, it wasn't true, the next year a few more were found flourishing in a different body of water. This summer several of the crawling fish were found in another source of water in Virginia. Creepy, I know. Is it possible that some year soon a multitude of Snakehead fish will be discovered in the Bay devastating an already depleted ecosystem stuffing themselves on crabs? After looking at a menu somewhere one day, will we wonder what this new fish called a Chesapeake Bay Striped Rainbow Fish tastes like? Would you feel the same way if you knew you were about to devour a Snakehead? That's why I say eat more lobster and save the fish. Or else you might be plunking down chunks of change to get a taste of the Chesapeake Bay Striped Rainbow Fish and feel privileged.

Rando if you do know (III)

THE DRIFTER

Mack's retirement plan is watching driftwood come ashore. He reckons some days he'll have to float wood himself to stay entertained.

TARCOCK THEORY

If Puerto Rico ever joins the United States as a state, then the best option to keep the symmetry of having fifty states, instead of fifty-one and thus saving the cost of remaking all those flags, rewriting all those books, websites, and other texts might simply be to combine the states of North Carolina and South Carolina into one grand ole state called Carolina.

Right now, citizens of both states refer to their Carolina as the true Carolina anyway. North Carolina might be slightly more famous because of its basketball team thanks to Michael Jordan. But the Gamecocks served not too long ago as a semi-consistent football powerhouse in the SEC after so many years of languishing as a subpar team. At least when Jadevon Clowney played and before Steve Spurrier abandoned them. And then there's National Champ Clemson: BOO! Eat a burger.

Starting with the Lost Colony never to be found by Sir Walter Raleigh for which the NC capital has been named, the Carolinas have been quintessential to American history be it in killing the Native Americans, enforcing racism, slavery, starting the Civil War, perpetuating Appalachia stereotypes, hosting many a soldier for training at Ft. Bragg or Paris Island or many others. And still the two states have tried to be separate entities denying that they should be together since their split in 1712. It's time to forgive.

A United Carolina, named after Charles I of England, existed before. Well whatever, at least they got that taxing British burden off their backs later, but there was a rift and North and South divided essentially along the lines that still exist today. Sure, they fought side by side and continued to share a lot in common like people and accents and mountains and rivers and the Atlantic. Still, they were viewed as different, but they never fought. Right?

So, then it's overdue to reconnect and make a mega state to compete with the best of the best. It could be the California of the East. But it can't be the Tarheel State, nor the Gamecock State (Palmettos?). And no one would ever think to associate Carolina with Tigers or Blue Devils to name a few fiends within.

No, the two realistic options are Gameheel or Tarcock. Gameheel doesn't make sense, nor does the Tarcock, and certainly not Tarmetto. But if you dig deeper, perhaps Tarcock does. The Tarheel concept supposedly came about during one of the old wars when the boys from North Carolina held their ground in battle. It was like they had tar on their heels. See?

So maybe Tarcock is too sexual for some. But that's a misinterpretation. And that's nothing new with a word involving cock. I've met more than one person wearing a Cocks hat who never heard of USC, unless you're talking Trojans.

No, the Tarcock would be a mighty chicken that stands its ground. A great metaphor for overcoming fear itself.

The legend of the Tarcock began sometime on the Cape Fear River. Somehow the Tarcock was always on the right side of history: offering cures to Native Americans for smallpox; providing food and shelter to runaway slaves; neutralizing the Klan; empowering Appalachians; running fair elections; reducing environmental burdens of pigs; and stopping hurricanes. All Carolina problems somewhat solved by the Tarcock. Who knew?

This Tarcock could be a great symbol for Carolina when it becomes a state. Some might argue for a naming contest, or something that may never cause offense as has been done when replacing mascot names associated with Native Americans. For example, the Newberry College Indians (why?) became the Newberry College Wolves (meh?) in 2008. Somehow the Catawba College Indians kept their name. Great river by the way, flows through North and South Cackalacky.

There needs to be a common cause to unite Carolinians, and there will certainly be a fear to face and overcome with unification. Sure, there may be some nervous people like when Germany reunited. Of course, this isn't volatile Korea or Timor. No, it's stable, but many questions will be raised. And they will be addressed in due course once unified, not now, and there's nothing finer than to be in Carolina, as they say, at least in the morning.

To overcome this fear, there needs to be the unifying concept of the Tarcock. And what say you of the many people not affiliated with these two universities that go well beyond this within Carolina. There are many other great institutions within the mega state. Sure, but we are inundated with images of

Tar Heels and Gamecocks, so Carolinians are used to this imagery. And hence, such combined imagery of a Tarcock should continue. This will no doubt boost economic output and production and perhaps even create jobs at the new Tarcock factory.

You may recommend one of the professional team names, but would you? They're all lame: Panthers, Hurricanes, Bobcats (sorry Mike that was the best name you could come up with?).

Other issues of contention could be settled like how do you pronounce B-E-A-U-F-O-R-T? Some say phonetically Bew while others say Bo. Going forward it could be Bewo-fort.

The Tarcock could lead an agricultural campaign to plant more peaches and less tobacco.

Recipes for bar-b-que could remain an issue. But this is easily solved as there are already long-established separations between East and West on preparations and sauces in bar-b-que, so there is plenty more range to keep up friendly smoked meat rivalries. Have a bite, Tarcock style.

Charlotte would probably be the capital. Although, personally, I'd suggest nearby Rock Hill, despite being like the only place anywhere to ban MTV. But Raleigh and Columbia could maintain their ranks as decent, yet dull places to live. Charleston and Asheville would retain their charms and benefit from a combined brochure offering the best of both the sea and the mountains all in one state instead of two or something like that. Anyway, the Tarcock State is something to consider: First in Flight with Smiling Faces and Beautiful Places. Make it happen Carolina.

WHO'S AFRAID OF WEENIE MCMANUS?

WEE BAIRN

The wee bairn born in the barn wasn't a bear at all.
It was a boar!

Weenie McManus was a three-foot one-inch man-child at age twenty-four. He resembled a large toddler with curly blonde locks and bright blue eyes.

Blue eyes, if you saw them, but the mask tended to get in the way. Afflicted since birth, Weenie's condition precluded him from breathing fresh air and developing as a typical human.

Dr. Procliff, a perceptive doctor, realized Weenie's disease early enough to catch it. Weenie suffered from a rare disease eventually known as Proclifferitis. Weenie was the only person known to survive the disease.

Proclifferitis occurs when the parasite of the female Ghanaian dust mite called the *p. vavinas* enters the bloodstream of an expectant mother after taking one of the dust mite's eggs on its back. Weenie's mother worked as a missionary in Accra when Weenie was conceived. Unbeknownst to even the most scientific observer, the *p. vavinas* somehow travels through the mother's bloodstream following a Ghanaian dust mite bite until *p. vavinas* reaches the fetus during the second trimester. The Ghanaian dust mite develops inside the fetus.

Upon giving birth the mother dies instantly and the baby always followed six minutes later. There was no way to detect *p. vavinas* the Ghanaian dust mite, until Weenie McManus.

Orphaned at birth and a ward of the state until eighteen, Weenie spent his youth confined to a small hospital room with no windows where he was observed by various medical students of Dr. Procliff.

A few years later Dr. Procliff developed the special mask that Weenie wore, which gave him a certain amount of freedom to walk around. Soon after the novelty of being able to leave the hospital abated, Dr. Procliff's research grants expired. Rumors soon turned to allegations which led to retractions of falsified lab reports in several distinguished medical journals. Forced to resign, Dr. Procliff lost his license to practice medicine.

Weenie needed a job.

"I tell you that Weenie McManus is after my job," Carl said before taking a sip of his whiskey. "They're phasing me out with that damned new smelting technique with the smaller pipe fitting."

Carl's job involved crawling through a narrow pipe full of toxic fumes and flipping a switch every twenty minutes for the smelting processes consistency to remain intact. Someone had to do it.

"What are you talking about Carl," Gus asked. "You're the only one that can flip that switch. Who else is going to get into that tiny crawl space and flip the switch to start the process?"

"Weenie McManus, that's who," Carl said. "That little shit's a foot shorter than me and they gave him that custom-made mask filter for the system. I'm screwed."

Rando if you don't know (XIII)

ABSOLUTELY
No,
nope,
naw,
not really,
meh,
sorta,
kinda,
maybe,
yeah,
yes!

BLEAKY

Deep underground in the Port Authority Bus Terminal miserable faces formed a line next to a worn-out door waiting on an express bus one hour and forty-seven minutes late. A large unavoidable clock ticked away the seconds irritating the line. Other travelers milled about the terminal going to and from destinations across the northeast and greater America.

The would-be passengers' nerves frayed with the anxiety of standing frozen on line in the subterranean catacombs of Manhattan.

The terminal smelled of old bacon, stale sweat, and spoiled fruit. The ventilation failed to blow in any sense of fresh New York City air.

A few vendors hawked their wares, including a short, stout Latino man offering the latest pirated copies of DVDs. No one chose to peruse his blockbusters on his fourth attempt at selling to the same tired line that only wanted to board their bus.

Staff members from the Standard Bus Company stood by the door acting as gatekeepers impeding freedom and progress. They mainly averted their eyes to avoid the cold stare of the line, or answered a similar query over and over again. "Where's the bus?" They didn't know when the bus would arrive, they said. There had been some mechanical problems, and, no, a replacement bus was not being offered nor a refund.

Two young men joked about making a run for the door saying they bet the bus was waiting and ready to go. With a little more age and stronger voices, they may have led the charge beyond the door to freedom or at least to the suffocating, fumy area where the arriving and departing buses rumbled. The thought piqued the interest of several line members, including Preston Young.

Preston, like the others, but all with different reasons, stared off vacantly with a hint of anger and annoyance welling up between his shoulder blades. A flurry of massages for the entire line would have worked a treat. Where were those hassling people offering ten-minute massages at street fairs when you needed them?

Closer to thirty than twenty, Preston scratched at the few days' growth of patchy dark stubble on his face. His short hair appeared disheveled. He'd woken up from a late evening nap when he got the news, and took off for the Port Authority immediately. A worn-out polo shirt and brown chinos covered his lanky frame. He thought they made him look cool, but someone with a keener fashion sense might have noted that the chinos were out of style by at least two years.

Preston craved a cigarette, but dared not give up his spot in the line. He imagined using the bottom of one of his red Pumas to stub out a cigarette with satisfying completion. He regretted drinking a large cup of coffee. At such an hour, the caffeine wired him for the misery of the line and hotly stirred his bowels. He hoped that whenever the bus arrived, the bathroom onboard worked.

Suddenly the door to freedom shot open, and a large man with dusty safety goggles, gloves, and a walkie-talkie emerged with a scowl. He chatted for a few moments with the other S.B.C. staff members leaving the door to freedom ajar for the line to gaze at desperately in false hope. No bus appeared. The goggled man laughed with the other staff members. Perhaps they enjoyed the misery of the would-be passengers. Then safety goggles slammed the door shut, and left responding to a scratchy, muddled voice coming from his walkie-talkie.

The two-hour mark passed without solution. Quips of discontent grew more frequent and vocal. An older black man suggested everyone should get a free ticket to the staff members, but their eyes simply shot away towards the bagel stand offering no response.

As time dragged, Preston questioned why he hadn't opted for the train. He could be deep into Jersey already. Instead, he stood plagued with a desire for the toilet, unwilling to relinquish his spot in a line that led to nothing, yet grew ever longer. More and more people expecting to catch the bus to the same destination every hour on the half-hour wondered where the fabled bus out of New York might be.

Preston's lower abdomen rumbled in anguish forcing him to distract his body from losing control of his bowels in a very public place. He counted the number of bricks in the wall and intermittently reread for the fourth time the free newspaper that he'd picked up near his subway stop. The circumstances forced him to feign interest in reading intently about some washed up celebrity's latest gasp for attention. Preston's forehead began to sweat. He pondered losing it, and which first, his mind or his bowels.

Finally, right when Preston thought his pants might soil, the door to freedom opened and the bright lights of a bus shined. Tired and worn passengers disembarked gathering their things likely relieved to at last be in the Big Apple.

The line to freedom began to move. Being closer to the front Preston only had to wait for sixteen people to offer their tickets for punching by the driver and optionally stow their bags in the undercarriage.

Soon Preston stood in front of the pudgy, crusty, mustachioed, balding, cheap-cologne-wearing bus driver in a faded blue uniform. The driver grunted, while tearing the ticket, and motioned him towards the bus door.

Preston's light baggage precluded him from the undercarriage. He quickly climbed the steps into the cold air-conditioned bus, which shook and rumbled thanks to its diesel engine and poor maintenance record.

Preston carefully waded his way towards the back of the darkly lit interior avoiding passengers settling into their claimed seats.

Preston eventually made it near the back where he threw his bags on a seat and rushed to the bathroom at the rear. At first, the door refused to open. He worried he might be stuck on the bus for God knew how long with the desperate need to send some logs down the river. Preston noticed the door was locked. He waited by rocking unsteadily back and forth. But soon the door opened, and a fat white man emerged and awkwardly rounded past Preston, who eagerly rushed into the bathroom.

Preston shut the door quickly and a dim light came on. He didn't mind the deep smell of disinfectant, but the spots of urine sprayed all over the toilet seat by the previous occupant deterred his progress. Preston wanted to sit instantly as his bowels loosened, however, he decided to speedily wipe the seat and then build a nest with the abundant roll of toilet paper.

Upon sitting, a satisfying feeling came over him as relief dropped by to say hello. He finished his deeds and washed up. That's when the strong disinfectant clogged his olfactory senses. He glanced momentarily in the mirror at his tired eyes. After some other desperate passenger knocked on the door, he quickly exited.

Preston couldn't remember what seat he threw his bags on. He found them a few rows up in a right window seat next to a woman who looked early thirties, wearing light brown cowboy boots, a blue jeans skirt above the knees, and a loose white top that may have been purchased in India. He smiled and excused himself pointing to his seat. She got up. He brushed past her noting the flowery smell of her long black hair.

Preston felt the woman's gazing presence upon him as the bus rounded out the Port Authority and down into the Lincoln Tunnel. He grew anxious. Despite his best efforts to cast a brooding air by staring out the window, he couldn't help but start a conversation by the time they rose into New Jersey.

"Gosh that wait took so long, didn't it?" the woman said.

Preston nodded in agreement.

"I never thought we would get on," the woman said. "And then I was the last one to get on. I felt so sorry for those people who had to wait for the next bus. But I made it boy. They need to accommodate passengers more. What would they have done if we had to stand there all night long?"

"Nothing, if they don't have to," Preston offered. "This is the last time I ever have to take the bus."

"Oh, I don't know," the woman said. "I don't mind it. It's a lot cheaper than flying and I'm scared of flying. That's why I end up taking the bus so much. I try to go up to see some my friends in every month or so. Normally, it's four hours back to Baltimore. What about you? Where are you heading?"

"Richmond."

"Do you live there? I've never been, but I guess there's probably some charm to it, like any place, huh?"

"I guess so," Preston said. "Actually, I'm from a town outside of Richmond, but I've lived in the city for some time."

"Going home to see the parents?"

"Something like that," Preston said before creating an awkward pause.

Another moment passed, and the woman took it no more.

"My name is Danielle, what's yours?"

"Preston, nice to meet you," he said offering his hand. She shook it briefly and Preston noted how soft and smooth her hand felt.

"Where do you live, in Manhattan?" she asked with vigor.

"No, I live in Long Island City."

"Where's that?"

"It's in Queens."

"Oh, I've never been outside of Manhattan, even though I've been to New York, God knows how many times."

"They say Astoria is an up and coming area," Preston said. "Whatever that means, but it's not a place you would go unless you live there. I mean there are a few cool things in the neighborhood. Like there's a film studio out there called Silver Cup. And in the summers, there's this museum called PS 1 that opens up and throws a party on the week-ends with DJ's and beer. Plus, there's the Bohemian Beer Garden in Astoria in the summer too, but that's about it, unless you like Greek food."

"I do," Danielle said. "Maybe I'll get my friends to go out there the next time I'm up. What was it called again?"

"Long Island City or Astoria."

"And what do you do in Long Island City or Astoria?"

"Why live the New York City dream, of course," Preston said with a slight chuckle. "What do you do?"

He thought it best to turn the conversation back to her. If she delved too deeply, she might realize his meager means of being based in Queens. But heck, he thought, they were on a bus, she must be all right or a total nutjob.

"I'm a non-profiteer," she said telling what sounded like a well-worn line. It still got a wry smile.

"That's why you ride the bus. How do you not make money?"

"I work for an organization called Safe House that helps refugees resettle in America. We try to place refugees in housing around the area and set them up with work and a new life."

"Sounds interesting, and tough I bet?"

"Yeah, there are so many sad cases and so many people that we can't take in. The stories of suffering get to me sometimes. I wish I could help them all."

"Can't save the world all at once."

"No, but it would be nice, and it's been harder helping people with this crap about Homeland Security. That idiot Bush annoys me so much. All those stupid laws he got passed prevent so many desperate people from getting the help they need. Meanwhile, his rich cronies make out like bandits. Sorry I don't know you, and here I am rambling about politics."

"Preach on sister. You're in liberal company."

"Ugh, I could go on forever."

And she did. Not only about political viewpoints and the mental capacity of George W., but she talked for a long time with Preston gladly nodding and piping in a cute, quick quip here and there. Somehow the subject turned to drinking and Danielle's drunken night out with her good friends. Apparently, a friend was getting married. There was a bachelorette party. Several close friends of the bride, including Danielle, went on a huge bender. They got lashed and worked up the courage to go to a strip club. After dropping several bills in banana baskets, they giddily entered a twenty-four-hour adult boutique near Times Square.

"Somehow I ended up with this," Danielle said showing a key ring with a small plastic penis attached to it. "Jeez, I can't believe I'm showing you this, you must think I'm a total weirdo."

"Nah, strangers show me their penises on the bus all the time."

He'd seen worse than a wee dildo before, but questioned why she chose to share her mini phallus. Was she up for it? And if so where might they do anything? Certainly not in the seat, and no way could Preston be tempted back into the bathroom, even for the promise of sweet momentary bliss. Did buses ever stop at observation points in the night? Sadly no, and Danielle, who'd laughed richly at Preston's last comment, quickly quelled any prospects:

"Oh, you're funny. I hope I'm not leading you on," she said.

"The thought hadn't crossed my mind," Preston replied looking to the left. "So, what are your plans for that thing anyway?"

"I think I will carefully store it away somewhere special. Having it on my key chain in my pocket made me finally see what it must be like to be on the receiving end of the old is that something in your pocket or are you happy. Ya know?"

Preston laughed at that oldie but goodie.

Their conversation carried on again with Danielle leading the charge until they exited I-95 in Baltimore pulling into the bus station.

"Hey I know you probably don't want to give your number to a total stranger, but if you want to meet next time you're in the big city," Preston said.

"Sure, yeah that would be great," she said reaching into her bag to grab a pen and scrap of paper. "Besides you're not a stranger anymore Preston. What's your number?"

Preston provided his digits, which Danielle dutifully jotted down. She scrawled her number on another piece of paper and handed it to him. Then the bus came to a stop. After gathering her things Danielle offered her hand to Preston who returned the favor. They shook hands briefly. Rather unexpectedly Danielle dotted a quick peck on Preston's cheek before offering a smile, bidding adieu, and quickly exiting the bus.

Wow what was that for, Preston wondered. He felt good to have had a chat with a cool woman along the way. He could not help but smile as he looked out the window and watched Danielle gather her bags from the undercarriage with the help of the bus driver. His thoughts drifted back to his preoccupation.

Any brief feeling of bliss changed to discomfort as a new male passenger weighing 300-plus pounds sat next to him with no "excuse me" offered. Instead only a grunt followed by continuous heavy breathing, loud enough to be considered a waking snore. The fat man's body flopped into the seat taking more than the slender amount of comfort provided by the narrow single seat. Pegged against the window, Preston tried to avoid touching the fat man's body, which protruded far over into his seat. It was impossible, and Preston gave in contemptuously resting his shoulder against the blubber. The heat, from the fat man's body touching his, warmed Preston quickly in a most uncomfortable way with no chance of escape until he changed buses in Washington D.C. It should take an hour, right?

An unexplained traffic jam pushed the journey to D.C. closer to two hours. Sweat frosted by the chill of the AC tinged the tips of Preston's hair. The heat oozed off the fat man onto him. He felt nauseous. He wanted to retrieve the bottle of water from his bag, which he had foolishly stowed in the overhead compartment.

Pinned in, he couldn't move a quarter of his torso. The fat man slept peacefully never stirring even when Preston forcefully attempted to switch positions to no avail.

The torturous ride eventually ended as they rolled into the dimly lit D.C. station. The fat man continued sleeping. Preston fretted that he might never exit the bus. He rationalized the need to scream.

"HEY!" he yelled into the fat man's ear.

One or two more screams caused the other exiting passengers to turn their heads toward the back. Suddenly, the fat man turned and looked into his eyes with a groggy look.

"Oh, excuse me, is this your stop, honey," an angelic voice asked.

Preston shrieked internally before saying: "Yes, pardon me."

It felt great to stretch and walk around after leaving the bus. Then the stifling summer humidity crushed the night and any rejuvenating spirit Preston attained. He entered the bus terminal to check the departures screen to see the next for Richmond. A journey from New York to Richmond should take five hours; that is without any issues. With the delay and traffic, Preston was already in hour eight with at least two more hours depending on when and if he could catch a Richmond bus.

Preston's tired eyes gazed at the departures screen trying to discern if a bus existed. No mention of Richmond appeared. He approached the information counter finding a mug that clearly wanted to be elsewhere, but dutifully answered the same queries over and over again.

"Excuse me," Preston said clearing his throat. "Where's the bus to Richmond? It's not on the screen."

"You were on that late bus, huh?" the station agent blubbered.

"Yeah."

"You just missed the last bus for Richmond. The next one doesn't leave until 6:15 am that's why it's not on the screen."

"6:15am!"

"Yep."

"Shit! Sorry. Thanks."

Preston stepped outside to smoke. He checked his phone to see he had one missed call. He knew who it would be, but figured it was too late to call. He thought about calling a friend in California to kill some time, but realized his battery would soon die. Gotta save the juice, he thought. Besides, it had been a long time since he spoke with his friend last, what could he say.

The woody flavor of smoke and the rush of nicotine to his brain woke Preston. He surveyed his surroundings and realized why most people avoided taking the bus if possible. The atmosphere was bleak, un-American. Almost no one wanted to be there, but the need to travel a distance at an affordable price required it for most of those in attendance. For others the station was a necessity for a place to call home and bathe. Several skeevy characters of various extractions loitered around the parking lot in an intimidating manner.

Halfway through Preston's cigarette, a man, who practiced poor hygiene, perhaps not by choice, stepped in front.

"You got an extra smoke?" the man inquired.

"Sure," Preston said pulling out his pack. He opened it and handed the man a cigarette.

"Can I get a light too?"

"Yeah," Preston responded, while digging in his pocket. A hole had developed in the left pocket of his chinos, which made him keep all of his change on the right side. Of course, he understood this after walking to the laundromat sometime back and all of his quarters spilled onto the sidewalk. At any rate, the hole had grown and nearly caused the lighter to fall down his pants. He dug and dug. The man waited with an uncertain look as Preston reached in his pants.

Finally, Preston came out with the lighter and lit the man's cigarette.

"Thanks buddy," the man said. "Say, friend, I don't suppose you could lend an old vet a few bucks to get a meal?"

"Sorry, no I can't."

"All right, thanks for the smoke," the man said before walking over to another bystander and asking for change.

Preston didn't mind giving out cigarettes figuring it increased the chances of getting one if in need. Smoky karma. However, any sympathetic sense of doling out money to bums quickly escaped his mind thanks to living in New York.

He threw the remains of his cigarette in a wet spot on the parking lot's tarmac before reentering the terminal.

Comforting wary travelers along their journey was not a consideration of the bus terminal designers. A few people slept in the uncomfortable bubble chairs dating back to the 1960s, which provided strong metal arm rests so no one could lie down. Most people occupying the seats stared off blankly somewhere or read, while a few conversed with others.

Generally, the terminal was quiet late at night. Or was it morning? Preston wondered checking the clock. 3:17am. He found the snack area, which consisted of several vending machines offering unhealthy, sugar-coated fare. He slowly sifted through his right pocket for change and came out with enough to buy a can of cola and a sticky honey bun.

Finding a vacant seat in the corner, he snapped the tab on the cola can and gulped before unwrapping the bun to take a huge chomp. All the sugar pumped him up with false energy or provided enough alertness so that he couldn't doze off. He spent the rest of the night contemplating his life past, present, and future between and during cigarette breaks. It was mostly bleak.

At last a scruffy voice announced over a speaker out of view that the bus bound for Richmond was ready to board.

By the time they rolled over the Potomac, Preston hoped to be sound asleep, but his thoughts encompassed any attempts at deep rest.

Arriving in Richmond, Preston pulled out his phone. The battery must have died in the night. He had no juice. Crap, he thought, and scrounged in his pocket for change. A local call cost fifty cents. When was the last time he used a payphone, he thought. He didn't have the change and had to ask a newspaper vendor to make some. He also bought a copy of *The Richmond Times-Dispatch* thinking he might have to wait a while. He was too tired to glance at the headlines making his way back to the payphone. What was the number? He thought for a moment. How could he forget? He dialed and after a few rings a familiar voice answered.

Rando if you don't know (XIII.5)

FENCES

Hitting that neighbor who vandalized the rental property you live in lightly with a baseball bat, but no resolution.

Whoops, you say before walking away from the neighbor's angry bewilderment.

Later you find the fence broken, and wonder will you get your deposit back.

H&H

Henning and Hornbostle, or H&H, specialized in industrial magnets. Next to H&H's store in the Cedar Hills Shopping Experience, an outfit called Big Pine Sky sold outdoor adventure gear like items for camping, hiking, and fishing. The problem with this neighborly order was that sometimes late at night Cameron Henning of H&H tested industrial magnets at full strength creating a magnetic force that attracted metal within fifty feet.

Usually, the fifty-foot radius encircled the back middle of H&H's back room, but one night Henning was feeling woozy and paid no attention where he rolled his huge magnet. It was about twenty-five feet to the left of normal, and his assistant Betty was more focused on reading her horoscope when she flipped the switch to electrify the magnet.

Fully operational the magnet did what magnets do: attract metal. Henning hoped to see a large piece of metal from forty feet away be dragged to the magnet plus a smaller piece at a different angle. The magnetic attraction worked as Henning watched the pieces move closer to the magnet and speed up in the nearing process when he turned up the force. A loud clank started next door at Big Pine Sky.

The magnet's force drew all outdoor products with metal toward it, including a case of knives that didn't fly in the air, but instead slid on the ground and in the process sliced up a prized $3000 rubber raft. An aluminum canoe also skated across Big Pine Sky's floor slowly wreaking havoc as it was pressed to the wall, which stopped all items in Big Pine Sky from making it over to H&H but caused that loud clanking noise.

Henning and Betty stirred from their stations. Realizing their error, they thought it best to turn off the magnet and put it in storage.

The next morning, Henning received a call from Dan the manager at Big Pine Sky asking for an explanation, saying that most of Big Pine Sky's merchandise was ruined. Big Pine Sky couldn't open, and Dan didn't know if insurance covered the damages, did Henning know what happened?

Henning played dumb speculating teenage vandals.

Dan countered that why would vandals take all metal products in the entire store and put them against the wall right next to the magnet store, but not steal a thing.

Henning was excited that his efforts to increase the magnetic power worked, but also alarmed. He had no way to pay for Big Pine Sky's damages. Hornbostle had been a silent partner prone to drunkenness at best, often heavier stuff, so there would be no help.

Henning decided rather than deny it, to say that Dan should file a claim with insurance and that he didn't like the tone Dan was taking.

Dan said he wasn't taking a tone; it was a simply obvious about the magnets.

To which Henning suggested Dan talk to H&H's lawyer Barry Cohen.

Lawsuits, countersuits, and many motions were filed. Media became informed, as well as the general public that especially loved the items for sale at Big Pine Sky and not so much at H&H. Although H&H sold a steady stream of kitchen magnets, but few industrial strength magnets that made the big money.

Henning knew cash-strapped H&H couldn't make it past the holiday season without going way up in sales because Barry's fees were so high and there was the real risk that they would lose the suit filed against them because Big Pine Sky's lawyer had subpoenaed electricity bills that more or less verified what was known and which Henning and Betty up to that point denied happened.

Namely, that the big magnet was misplaced and attracted all of the metal gear in Big Pine Sky until the force destroyed the shop.

Then a Big Pine Sky lawyer got to Betty. She flipped for fear of perjury charges. Also, only being paid minimum wage keeps one but so loyal.

A magnet expert also convinced the jury about the power of the modern magnets speculating that H&H must have known.

Big Pine Sky was ruined and H&H was ruined. As two of the anchor stores of the Cedar Hills Shopping Experience, the losses dealt a death blow to the debt-ridden shopping enter. Big Pine Sky won against H&H, but the magnet company was already bankrupt by then. Henning was off to find magnets in nature and Hornbostle died from pancreatic cancer.

Only Barry benefited by banking various legal fees. And in the end the magnet disaster helped James Hitchens get elected as a state senator because he said he would sponsor a bill banning magnet stores from being within 200 feet of any store containing metal. This meant that magnet stores went out of business and setback the home industrial magnet industry by decades. Home electric magnets were out and many citizens up in arms questioned why anyone ever wanted such a device.

Rando if you do know (IV)

SLOW

You go slow!
What do you know?
You go slow, slow, slow.
And then you go!

BLACK JEANS

A Raida B song contest:

> Walking downtown
> Tryin' to hide my frown
> Feeling so sad
> Cause my jeans are dookie brown
> Forget the rants
> Change my pants
> Everybody needs a black pair of jeans

Drum break tatatststststddfssaa

> Big party what to wear
> Black jeans new pair
> Feeling good,
> Feeling right
> Not too loose,
> Not too tight

Everybody needs a black pair of jeans

Drum break tatatststststddfssaa

Put em on
Everybody
Black jeans

Hotel lobby
Seeing hotties
Black jeans

Red carpet
Oscar party
Black jeans

Airport hangar
Big jet
Black jeans

Sidewalk sale
Lots of deals
Black jeans

Coffee shop
Double latte
Black jeans

Put em on
Everybody
Black jeans

Everybody needs a black pair of jeans

Drum break tatatstststststddfssaa

Tattoo parlor
Fresh ink
Black jeans

Pizza ordered
Extra cheese
Black jeans

Watching TV
With my family
Black jeans

By the pool
No running
Black jeans

Walking Rover
Doggie Park
Black jeans

Put em on
Everybody
Black jeans

Everybody needs a black pair of jeans

Drum break tatatstststststddfssaa

With my lady
On my knees
Black jeans

Broken windows
So sorry
Black jeans

Grocery store
Chocolate milk
Black jeans

In my car
New Ferrari
Black jeans

Out fishing
Nothing biting
Black jeans

Put em on
Everybody
Black jeans

Everybody needs a black pair of jeans

Drum break tatatststststddfssaa

Tossing salad
Kitchen counter
Black jeans

Big project
Due tomorrow
Black jeans

On the bus
Crazy driver
Black jeans

Farmers market
Ripe tomatoes
Black jeans

Reading news
Skewed views
Black jeans

Put em on
Everybody
Black jeans

Everybody wants a black pair of jeans

Everybody finds a black pair of jeans

Everybody gets a black pair of jeans

Everybody has a black pair of jeans

Put em on
Everybody
Black jeans

Everybody wears a black pair of jeans

Drum break tatatststststddfssaa

STRANGE WOOD

In an ancient city where mysteries happened before, Jacob walked up an enclosed wooden tunnel, where two policemen stood arresting some big guy. The police blocked Jacob's way. He skirted around. Then the whole floor and walls moved fast.

Vortexed, suddenly, Jacob turned upside down on a rickety wooden rail cart on a track carrying him fast over the city. Riding the upside down highline, the cart suddenly stopped. As the only passenger, Jacob discerned he must get down. To do so meant jumping out on to a chain-link ladder with no protection and a fifty-foot drop. He hesitated. The cart moved on. With no choice, he reluctantly jumped to the ladder, held tight, then slid down like a breeze.

Before, his slide, Jacob faced a huge skyscraper outside the wooden city.

The Commander and his entourage worked inside a big, spacious elevator car with a special desk in the center for the Commander flanked by aides in special support stools. Jacob intervened or maybe interrupted some nuclear expert's mention of a bomb. It was urgent. Jacob joined the elevator party. They shot up quickly. Jacob recalled an office complex in the building with many stairs and red carpets.

Jacob thought of Miguel, and then Miguel appeared a minute later.

The same thing happened a week before. For whatever reason, Jacob thought of Ava and then she sat in the coffeeshop about two minutes later. They'd waved. Jacob hoped to figure out if he could harness this power, how to use it, and why. He never believed in coincidences.

Rando if you don't know (XIV)

ABSOLUTELY, NOT
Yes,
yeah,
maybe,
kinda,
sorta,
meh,
not really,
naw,
nope,
no!

NATURE KING

Bells ring from the gusts of wind. Hey, dance on air bushes. Weaving tree limbs. Bouncing. Two notes beat the notion of it all. Sounds resend or rescind. And the Nature played on. DJ Trev's concept involved recording winds blowing through forests. Then he produced and edited the recordings with heavy production values. Speed the sounds up to natural dance anthems, nature tones, and the dance for land.

These beats, some critics said, DJ Trev stole from Nature. Some even said from God because God didn't recoup any royalty check when DJ Trev's latest track started blowing up through a growing list of marquee electronic dance music events.

DJ Trev began learning or blending more and more. Then "Night of their tornado" dropped with lyrics. The song broke through to the Master stream, to the mainstream for DJ Trev.

For about eight weeks in the autumn last year car radios, dance clubs, hay riders seeking moments in parks, and any legit public places blasted "Night of their tornado."

Lyrics included: *Got you by my side party. Merry go slowed down and around. Sped up, mixed up in every which way. Twister to the beat. Twist it. Twisted Tornado Tonight.*

DJ Trev earned next level fame or famosity, as he called it. His inability to produce music without Nature bothered him. He tried composing little ditties, but no originals compared to the sharpness of the natural remix.

Fans and critics called DJ Trev the "Nature king," which irked him. He worried he could never be original.

DJ Trev plotted about destroying Nature by fire for a good new song. He pondered calling it, "Scorched earth." But he didn't follow through, although maybe he wished he acted.

Because Nature fought back, naturally, via lawyers in the form of a non-profit with the mission of getting justice for Nature called Justice for Planet Earth and Nature (J4PEN).

An unprecedented court decision around that time judged that Nature, like a corporation, was an entity, like any individual, and thus had rights. Nature had plenty of grievances. J4PEN's law firm Deloitte, Briggs, and Huffmeyer (DBH) aka Nature's legal team, proved highly effective.

Talk ensued of Nature succeeding after filing suit against big food corporations for profiting and manipulating natural products. Energy companies settled out of court for large undisclosed amounts, admitting no wrongdoing and no faults, but some of these companies complied with paying Nature royalties on all energy products with payments ordered paid retroactively. This bankrupted many smaller energy companies, but the bigger ones had enough to get by and make appeals. The same held true for the beverage industry, amongst many other industries.

To that point, Nature's legal team succeeded.

DJ Trev continued to gain fame or infamy for stealing Nature's beats.

An intern at DBH named Theo Cumberfeld got drunk one night, and tried impressing some woman on the dance floor when "Night of their tornado" played. The woman didn't reciprocate Theo's staggering advance and slurry line of, "Hey, wanna get twisted with me?" She suggested that Nature King's songs weren't for bump and grind action, and that Theo should, "fuck off!" Theo felt scorned, in turn, by DJ Trev.

Theo brought an idea to his boss the next day hoping to land a job at DBH which was fast becoming one of the most successful and prestigious law firms in the land thanks to the Nature suits. DJ Trev aka Nature King had to get got, Theo surmised and his boss said, "Go for it."

After the suit was filed, one of the music news web headlines read: "Nature King troll toll."

Upon forcing DJ Trev to disclose his sound productions methods, DBH offered DJ Trev a take it or get sued to no end deal asking for 50 percent of all past and future proceeds to go to Nature. This was the DBH standard.

DJ Trev declined trying to negotiate a cheaper rate. Why not 15 percent? No.

At the trial DBH presented Nature's case from every angle. It was clear that DJ Trev would lose because Nature's sounds made up nearly all of DJ Trev's songs.

Pretty soon DBH became more successful. Nature earned huge coffers of wealth from all the times exploited by corporations. The grievances were limitless. Stocks plummeted. Biotech firms faced bankruptcy, amongst many other industries.

People spoke about going back to Nature, not for conservation purposes, but to destroy Nature or to at least steal its money. DJ Trev joined this anti-Nature contingent. No one booked him. The Nature lawsuit cost him everything, including the love of his life, Allie. She was there for the drugs and parties, not DJ Trev. He was to blind to see it.

Meanwhile, representing Water, DBH started suing everyone for general use, like transportation companies for cargo shipped by sea, or power companies using hydropower from dams, which DBH said was a form of torture for water. Every gallon of water used deserved backpay of at least pennies on the dollar, but it added up fast.

Nature's full-time trustee, DBH, on behalf of J4PEN, began being accused of hoarding Nature's earnings and mistreating Nature's wages, particularly after Theo became partner. It was an abuse of trust. Several other law firms brought forth a suit stating that DBH should not be Nature's trustee, as they had proven to be detrimental to the earnings of Nature.

Lawyers and judges, and perhaps the general public via the media, decided to take a different direction with Nature. Its earnings should be spent.

The law of the land should be adhered to, but not in Nature's interest, according to many. The call came to develop a deal whereby the government made interest off the growing Nature trust reaching into the quadrillions of dollars. Countersuits were filed, although it was never clear who was for or against Nature. Meanwhile DJ Trev spiraled into a heavily depressed remix of cocktails and drugs.

"Night of their tornadoes" was banned. DJ Trev mostly spent his days and nights listening to the wind. Eventually, it made him smile.

IN THE STICKS

The black car died along a lonely road fifty miles from anywhere. The frustrated driver exited the car after banging the steering wheel with his hands and yelling a series of expletives. He threw his suit jacket on the ground before popping the hood. Fuming smoke and the smell of smoldering plastic and melting metal billowed out. The driver unintentionally inhaled deeply and turned around covering his mouth in a failed attempt to control his hacking cough. He fell to his knees on the road's dirt shoulder. Recovering from the bad air he reached for his cellphone. No reception. More expletives poured from his mouth while he pounded his hands in the dirt. In the process he dropped his phone. He picked it up after regaining his composure only to discover the impact somehow caused a permanent power disruption. Furious he chucked the phone into the thick woods by the road. He turned and walked back to the car, planning to kick the tire but struck the metal hubcap instead, and then reeled backwards from the instant stinging pain his foot suffered.

Settling down again he reached for the door handle and found the door locked. The windows were up and the keys rested in the ignition. He screamed out furious expletives in anger and violently shook the car by lifting the handle up and down spastically. The hard, plastic door handle snapped off and the driver fell backwards landing hard against the tarmac.

Slow to rise the driver lay in mild hysterics wondering why he had taken the absurd shortcut in the first place. To save time, of course. He had places to go and no time for the desolate countryside. He needed to follow leads and make contacts. Why did his boss make him go so far for a miniscule sale? So what if the client was a longtime customer? The driver could have made ten sales in the city and suburbs.

To expedite his flight back to civilization he took a road suggested by an elderly local at the last gas station many leagues back. The elderly local claimed the shortcut would save the driver two hours' time. The drive involved crossing an abandoned military base condemned by toxic waste and the odd live ordnance. Sure, the shortcut was illegal, and rarely traversed as the elderly local explained, but the driver didn't care. He had to be somewhere other than Podunk.

After brushing off his dignity, the driver circled the car like a stalking beast searching for an entry. Every door and the trunk remained locked. He slapped his hands on the top of the car and buried his head in his arms in frustration. The sun beat down and the hot metal of the car's black surface burned slightly. The driver briefly relished in the singeing pain and watched his sweat droplets sizzle on the metallic surface. Faintly by staring into the car top the driver made out his reflection and the glare of the bright baking sun, which created a glare in his eyes. Spurs of strange colorful light entered his sight. He grew disoriented. He turned and sat down leaning in the car's shadows wondering what he should do. He was thirsty and licked the seeping sweat developing around his lips. The heat grew irritating and stifling. He felt he could chop through the humid air with his hands. There was a bottle of water in the car, but how to get to it and then what? He couldn't stay by the car. There was no telling when the next car might come along. It could be days, he felt. He loosened his tie and unbuttoned the buttons on his shirt to alleviate his overheating body. He looked over into the dried drainage ditch at the side of the road and noticed a large stick. He picked up the thick solid piece of wood. Holding the wood in his hands, he shook it and took a swing as if batting for a baseball. This will do, he thought.

He strode with confidence over to the driver's door.

After taking a deep breath, the driver held the wood up high. He bashed at the window, keen for a solution. He repeated his motions several times to no avail. The window remained intact. His anger boiled and his heart raced with vile fury. Expletives streamed forth. He resolved upon a new plan. With a crazed look in his eyes, he ran across the road with the stick. He paused and held the wood out before him. He breathed deeply.

Like a charging doughboy running with a bayonet, the driver erupted into a frantic sprint. Primal screams from his belly bellowed all the way while he dashed forward.

With his extreme momentum, he plunged the wood through the window upon impacting with the car. The wood shattered through and the driver banged violently against the car. The driver gripped his side and bent over to catch his breath. With a grimace he stood erect again and wiped the dripping sweat from his brow. He turned around with a brief feeling of elation upon viewing his triumph.

Eager to get inside he carelessly reached through the hole in the window and scraped his arm deep against the shards of broken glass. Droplets of blood seeped from his abrasions to mingle with the thick flow of sweat rolling down his right arm.

Only after opening the door, the driver noticed the stream of blood. He yelped in pain seeing several shards imbedded in his right arm. In vain, he tried to remove the shards. Instead, he drove them deeper. He felt a strange tear in his arm.

That's not good, the driver rationalized. A gush of blood spewed forth. The blood quickly soaked pieces of his clothing with thick coats of red.

Frantic, the driver took off his shirt and attempted to swathe the gaping wound. Binding his tourniquet tighter with his belt, he believed he had stemmed the blood flow to a trickle. The right arm felt limp and immobile. Working through his new seething pain, his dry salty mouth reminded him of his original intent for the bottle of water. Using his left hand, he opened the car door fully and leaned inside to retrieve the bottle of water. Holding the bottle with his left hand he unscrewed the top with his mouth. Greedily, he guzzled the bottle of water. Temporarily satiated he leaned back against the car.

He passed out.

Flies began buzzing around his limp arm attracted by the sweet smell of coagulated blood. Stirring, he felt too weak to fend them off and looked up at the sun whose rays inundated him with stifling heat. The front seat contained shards of glass that the driver felt too fatigued to trifle with removing. He decided to lie in the back of the car to determine his next action and attempt to escape the flies by shutting the door.

The flies soon discovered the shattered window and flew in mass towards the driver's wound. The buzzing noise and the insulating heat of the car grew too strong to ignore. He exited the car and dashed around to the passenger side of the car hoping to find the last vestige of shade from the scorching sun.

What could he do, he pondered, between winces of pulsing pain. The car clearly wouldn't start. In either direction there was no sign of humanity. The thick woods on either side of the road looked impenetrable. Who knew what dangers lay inside. He slunk against the car certain he would die in this miserable lonely place of nowhere. He wanted to live, but had no recourse to his current plight. He began to cry. He felt pathetic and compromised by the surrounding elements.

Hours passed and the driver stared vacantly into the woods feeling faint from loss of blood and dehydration. The penetrating sun subsided as dusk drew near and the air steamed from the day's heat. The sounds of insects and animals starting to engage in their nighttime activities encroached upon the driver's ears. Stinging mosquitoes left welts on the driver's sweaty hot body, but he paid them little attention feeling too weak to feign concern. His vision faded in and out of the encompassing darkness of night.

Nodding back into the realities before him, the driver caught a glimpse of a light out of the corner of his eye. He wondered if it was the light that would perhaps lead him to heaven or hell. He stirred in an attempt to fight the light and turn away from it. The light kept coming faster and closer. Belonging to a rumbling truck, the light shone right upon the driver. A voice asked the driver if he was okay. No, the driver retorted and looked up to see a man in military fatigues. The military man asked the driver why he was there. The driver weakly replied, "a shortcut." The military man mentioned something about the area being federal property, but then noticed the driver's wound. Rushing forward to attend to the driver, the military man exclaimed that the driver needed medical attention immediately. The military man pulled the driver up from the side of the car and lugged him to the truck. Sitting in the passenger seat, the driver felt a sense of relief and hope as he took a big gulp of water from the canteen the military man passed him. The military man shifted the big truck into first, saying he would take him to the hospital.

Feeling refreshed, the driver asked the military man their destination.

The military man said Podunk.

Rando if you don't know (XV)

THE BAND

The thing with the band is there is no band. There never was a band. Some musicians played with me: the creative force behind the band. I wrote the music and the lyrics to every song. I played all the instruments on the recorded tracks. Hell, I even designed the cover art for the first album. I was the fucking band!

THINKING ABOUT IT

Thinking about it . . . what?
Thinking about it . . . where?
Thinking about it . . . when?
Thinking about it . . . who?
Thinking about it . . . how?
Thinking about it . . . why?
Because I'm thinking about it . . . when?
Thinking about it . . . who?
Thinking about it . . . what?
Thinking about it . . . how?
Thinking about it . . . who?
Thinking about it . . . why?
Because I'm thinking about it . . . where?
Thinking about it . . . how?
Thinking about it . . . who?
Thinking about it . . . when?
Thinking about it . . . what?
Thinking about it . . . why?
Who, what, where, when, why, how, now, wow!
Because I'm thinking about it.

BACKPACKING

Climb a tower.
Hike a trail.
See a church
to no avail.
What I seek?
I do not know.
On through Europe (or insert another place)
I must go.

Rando if you do know (V)

YOUTH HOSTEL SPONGE

Misuse of a worn youth hostel kitchen sponge leads to a
butter knife fight. A Canadian loses an eye and a Span-
iard flees Australia, while two Dutchies weep, or were
they Danes? They weep not for the Canadian, but the lost
margarine. A Kiwi consoles them, while a German walks
in late with a Swede unaware until noticing blood on the
floor and asks the Aussie clerk, "What has happened," to
which the clerk replies, "Crikey!"

TUMMY TIME

Fussin' and a cussin'
Fightin' and a feudin'
Just flip over and change your mind
Tummy time
Right on time
It's tummy tummy tummy tummy tummy time

Feeling good
Feeling fine
Just feel silly and change your mind
Tummy time
Right on time
It's tummy tummy tummy tummy tummy time

Feeling good
Feeling fine
Just flip over and change your mind
Tummy time
Right on time
It's tummy tummy tummy tummy tummy time

Not snack time
Not nap time
Not play time
It's tummy time
Right on time
It's tummy tummy tummy tummy tummy time

Feeling good
Feeling fine
Happy time
Funny time
Tummy time
Right on time
It's tummy tummy tummy tummy tummy time

Just be silly now change your mind
Tummy time
Tummy time
It's tummy tummy tummy tummy tummy time

It's tummy yummy funny tummy time
It's tummy tummy tummy tummy tummy time
It's tummy tummy tummy tummy tummy time
It's tummy yummy funny tummy time
It's tummy tummy tummy tummy tummy time
It's tummy tummy tummy tummy tummy time
It's tummy yummy funny tummy time
Tummy time, now flip!

QT BOWTIE LULLABIES

Go to sleep, little baby.
It's a good time to take a rest.
So your mom and your dad and Jakey Joe,
and grandma and grandpa and gran and auntie Mae,
and everyone else in the whole wide world
can do the things they need to do
to go to sleep too.
Like brush their teeth, read a book or watch TV
Maybe crochet, play cards or drink some tea.
So good night.
Good night.
It's time to turn out the light.
For the light is so bright,
and you see that it's night.
Well it must be all right.
So sleep tight.
Good night.
Enough all right.
No fret of a fright.
So good night.
Good night.
Don't let the spiders bite.
Good night!

EPILOGUE

The creepers creep and the beepers beep, but what about the leapers who leap? Or the deepers who deep and the steepers who steep? Why now is the red cow's milk so sweet and the butter of the black goat so blah? And if the black goat's butter is blah then shouldn't someone tell the black goat to change the formula? If these were the questions that had answers then we'd never be somewhere near to here that is so far and weird. A different verse in this universe or multiverse. Sometimes it rhymes, sometimes it mimes and mimics the truth of this world. My world, your world, our world, but it is its own. For who in our world ever thought butterflies would go fishing, but that's the truth in the world over there, where the mega monarch is a right good angler and the mini giraffe is the ideal candidate for landscaping services, particularly with old Scottish shrubberies. Tis a looming world in that many a wool is wound from looms and many a yarn is thread and told anew with colors unimagined and a science vast in possibilities we have only yet to comprehend or yet to see through a micro-telescope.

What is it I speak of you ask? Surely, this is the land of the as far as . . . It goes to a right galaxy so close and so far, as we know too far to go for we are too slow, and they maybe do not know or choose to look away from us for we are not enemies or friends. We are unbeknownst to them and them to us. Save for the few like us that may know too much but not enough to deliver the riddle of travel to the future where it is said our worlds collide and clash, and with destruction we bash and they bash until all there is little, save ash. But it may not have to be that way if you and I, and he and she, or the and they, and in between, if we together find a solution to my dilution and its method to take this bucket with us inside for a ride where we glide ever so quickly like the cheetah times one million billion cheating the odds and get there fast and first in a burst before our nemesis the Fake proceeds in a similar scam to take claim to the land of the golden sand clam. Let's go.

ABOUT THE AUTHOR

Doworth Howard is an underground writer and sculptor alive in the USA. When he's not writing or sculpting, he likes to take his dog Bailey for long walks on the beach and to town for snacks. He longed to be bicoastal now he's amid most all to somewhere neither here nor there.

www.ingramcontent.com/pod-product-compliance
Lightning Source LLC
Chambersburg PA
CBHW021711190726
48289CB00008B/2474